PEN
Bl

Dr Vineet Aggarwal is a doctor by qualification, manager by profession and artist by temperament. Born in a family of doctors, he successfully completed an initial stint with the family occupation before deciding to venture into pharmaceutical management. He pursues writing as a passion and is an avid travel photographer as well.

His literary repertoire extends from politics and poetry to travel and terrorism but his favourite genre remains the amalgamation of science and mythology. He is the author of the popular online blogs Decode Hindu Mythology and Fraternity against Terrorism and Extremism. This is his third book.

BY THE SAME AUTHOR

Vishwamitra
The Legend of Parshu-Raam

BHARAT

THE MAN WHO BUILT A NATION

DR VINEET AGGARWAL

PENGUIN BOOKS

An imprint of Penguin Random House

PENGUIN BOOKS

USA | Canada | UK | Ireland | Australia
New Zealand | India | South Africa | China | Singapore

Penguin Books is part of the Penguin Random House group of companies
whose addresses can be found at global.penguinrandomhouse.com

Published by Penguin Random House India Pvt. Ltd
4th Floor, Capital Tower 1, MG Road,
Gurugram 122 002, Haryana, India

Penguin
Random House
India

First published in Penguin Books by Penguin Random House India 2017

ISBN 9780143439981

Typeset in Minion Pro by Manipal Digital Systems, Manipal
Printed at Repro India Limited

www.penguin.co.in

MIX
Paper from
responsible sources
FSC® C047271

To all those who have fought for
the unity of our nation

Jai Hind

Vande Mataram

Contents

Contents

Author's Note

As someone once said, we live in interesting times.

If you look around and observe what's happening in the world you too will agree. The more our world is modified by technology, the more we seem to be regressing into age-old dogmas. Social media, that had invaded our homes with the promise of connecting people, has also become the biggest tool to divide those whose beliefs lie on the opposite end of the spectrum.

The old notions of liberalism, secularism and nationalism are fast changing form and people not just in India, but all over the world seem to be moving towards disintegration. In such a scenario, where can we take encouragement from? Perhaps we need to look into the past to find some inspiration. After *Vishwamitra* and *The Legend of Parshu-Raam*, this book is my attempt to bring to you the story of yet another inspiring man who not only brought the whole country together, but also gave it a new name—Bhaarat.

Many of you have heard the story of Dushyant and Shakuntala, the parents of Bharat, immortalized by the great Sanskrit poet Kalidasa. However, given the poetic license writers tend to take, the bard's version differs greatly from that given in the original Mahabharata. The initial part of my story is a unique blend of both, that cuts down the drama and brings more realism to the tale of Bharat's birth.

Besides being the son of two popular characters, Bharat was also the grandson of Brahmarishi Vishwamitra and Menaka, and a cousin of Parshu-Raam, believed to be an Avatar by many. The events in this book take place while the sixth incarnation of Vishnu is still roaming the world in his quest to wipe out corrupt and tyrannical Kshatriyas. This story is thus a sort of continuation of the stories of the other two men, though I have made a conscious effort to ensure that each of these books can be read by themselves as well.

When I was toying with the idea of doing a book on Bharat, I realized that there was hardly any information available about the man after whom our nation is named! Only a few details survive in the Mahabharata that tells the story of the descendants of Bharat. Even though we don't hear much about them now, the Bharat tribes are also extolled in the Vedas and were clearly greatly admired in ancient times.

According to popular lore, Bharat's empire is believed to have covered the entire Indian subcontinent, as well as Afghanistan, Bactria, Uzbekistan, Tajikistan, Kyrgyzstan, Turkmenistan and Persia. There are some accounts of his military exploits and he is believed to have defeated many foreign tribes such as the Kirātas, Hūnas, Yavanas, Kambojas, Paundras, Kankas, Śakas and others who were opposed to Vedic culture. It is these minor details, gathered from various sources, which form the basis of my plot.

This is the story of the man who brought our ancestors from various parts of the country under one banner. This is the story of the man who built a nation.

Prologue

He lay on the gargantuan coiled body of Shesha, the serpent of time. A golden dhoti draped his powerful legs while his muscular body, the colour of monsoon clouds, glowed with the effulgence of Brahma-jyoti. He wore no ornaments, save the Kaustubh gem that was obtained from the churning of the Ocean of Milk and now adorned his shapely neck. Ringlets of dark, curly hair spilled over a broad forehead, framing high cheekbones and lotus-bud eyes. Eyes that were even now dreaming the world into existence, spinning the web of life with his Yogmaya.

Shri Hari Vishnu, the Lord of All Creation, rested his handsome head on his right forearm, his other arms extended in various relaxed postures. His consort, Lakshmi, the goddess of fortune, leisurely wove a garland of vaijanti flowers. The Milky Way swirled languidly around their abode in Dhruv Loka, at the centre of the galaxy. Vaikunth was an oasis of peace in the misery of material existence, but its harmony was intermittently disturbed by the council of thirty-three Devas when things became too difficult for them to handle.

He was an integral part of the Holy Trinity of Creator, Preserver and Destroyer. Brahma fashioned things in the form of Srishti, and Shiva was responsible for Samhar or annihilation of all that had been created. And while the Creation existed, it was Vishnu's responsibility to maintain its Sthiti or equilibrium. But, things always had a way of unravelling themselves, a phenomenon known by the scientists of Swarg as 'Entropy'. This necessitated his intervention, an external balancing force.

Brahma's boons of conditional immortality were quite notorious, for they almost always led to a disturbance in the equilibrium between Good and Evil. In the very first hour of his present day, the Creator god had granted benedictions to Hiranyaksh and Hiranyakashyapu, the twin Daityas. These boons had resulted in widespread massacre of inhabitants of Swarg as well as Prithvi and Shri Hari Vishnu had been compelled to appear first as Varah and then as Narasimha to restore balance in the Three Worlds.

Shiva was not as indiscriminate as Brahma in granting boons. But he was also fair to a fault, and if suitably impressed, wouldn't think twice before showering even demons with immense powers. The Bhole-nath had once blessed Daitya-guru Shukracharya with the knowledge of reviving the dead, and again, it was Vishnu who had to help the Devas nullify the unfair advantage their opponents had. He suggested they churn the Cosmic Ocean to obtain Amrit, the elixir of immortality.

It had been an enormous task to convince the proud Indra to approach his arch-enemy Bali, the leader of the Asurs, and persuade him to help the Devas in the task. It had to be done in a way that the suspicion of the demons would not be roused. To everyone's relief Shakra, the current Indra, had managed to do so with aplomb. The two clans of divine beings had gathered to whip the Ocean of Milk using Mount Mandar as a churning rod but even that had been possible only after Vishnu balanced the mountain on his back in his Kurma, or turtle, incarnation.

The churning had provided them with unbelievable riches—Apsaras, the Kaustubh gem, the celestial cow Kamdhenu, the wish-fulfilling Parijat tree, the flying unicorn Ucchaishrava, the six-tusked elephant Airavat, and finally, Amrit. Again Vishnu intervened in the form of Mohini to make sure the Asurs did not get a single drop of the elixir, and distributed it amongst the Devas, thus restoring balance to the equation between the demigods and demons.

And such drastic interventions were required not only in the higher lokas but in the middle world as well. Vishnu had saved life on earth from extinction by taking the form of Matsya at the time of the Great Deluge. Ever since, he had been guiding humans in the forms of Nar-Narayan, Narad, Kapil and Dattatreya. He had appeared as Rishabhdev to teach the principles of civilization to humanity, and as Prithu to show mankind how to harness earth's resources, thus giving the planet its name: Prithvi.

More recently, he had blessed the young Brahmin son of Yamdagni with superhuman powers in order to neutralize the Asurik infestation that had spread over the world like a miasma. That boy, Parshu-Raam, had accomplished the task of eliminating the evil and corrupt kings from Nabhi-varsh and would soon head to other countries to fulfil his destiny. The Lord's vision filled with images of the young Brahmin boy utilizing his own divine bow and Shiva's axe to bring the evil plans of the Asur king Ravan to nought. He could see the young man blazing through the military hordes of nations like an inferno, bringing relief to the general populace, even as Ravan, the Asur who had begun the plague of darkness on earth, hid in the Himalayas trying to attain another boon from Shiva. Well, there was still some time before the prayers of that Brahmarakshas came to fruition.

As peace returned to Nabhi-varsh, the fates were conspiring to change the destiny of that land through another member of Parshu-Raam's family. Shakuntala, the daughter of Brahmarishi Vishwamitra and the Apsara Menaka, was going to be instrumental in reshaping her country's future. Vishwamitra had amazed the Trinity with his achievements before and there was no doubt that his offspring would do something momentous as well. The winds of change brewing on earth were going to transform things for all time to come.

The future was just beginning and Shri Hari Vishnu, the Preserver of Life, liked the direction it was taking.

Shakuntala

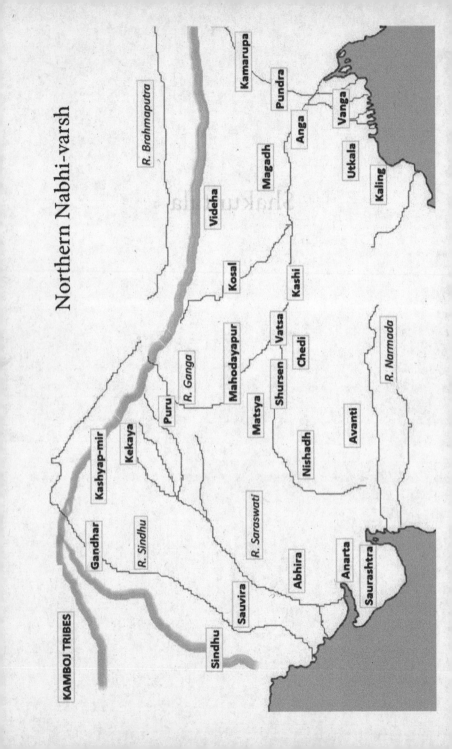

Northern Nabhi-varsh

Adhyaye 1

Voices filled the royal hall of Hastinapur, bouncing off the two dozen marble pillars that supported the high vaulted ceiling. Wide latticed windows provided illumination as well as ventilation to the cavernous hall that was full of people watching the royal debate.

Aileen, ruler of the Puru kingdom, sat on a beautifully carved sandalwood throne that had been fashioned to resemble the vehicle of the moon god, the founding father of the Chandravansh. It was shaped like a chariot drawn by eight antelopes, and the king occupied the central seat, sheltered by a silver umbrella. The elderly king was presiding over a debate between his eldest son and the royal council. Of his five sons, Dushyant, the eldest, was quite simply the best.

Since the day he had first stepped into the court, the crown prince had shown a flair for solving the tricky situations that arose in the running of a kingdom. Dushyant was almost twenty-five now, and towered over his sire. Aileen saw a glimpse of his own younger self in him; they had the same tan complexion, sharp nose and dark eyes but the king had a greying beard and his face had assimilated fine lines from years of looking after the kingdom, while his son's visage had the freshness of youth. Rigorous training had made Dushyant's body lithe like that of a cheetah and his mind as sharp as a needle. He was practical and perceptive, and even now seemed to be winning the debate that had almost reached its conclusion.

For more than a prehar now, the councillors and the prince had been debating the need to change old policies followed by the kingdom—three hours and counting. Aileen had been trying to get his council to formulate new guidelines for more inclusive development, but to no avail. Change was not easy for anyone, let alone senior members of the court who were set in their ways and accustomed to their lavish lifestyles, but the king hoped that his son would be able to convince them.

Rising to his full six feet, Dushyant addressed the assembly emphatically, 'The time has come for Hastinapur to introspect. We must decide which of our traditions are redundant and which can be retained. As the wielder of Shiva's axe, Parshu-Raam showed us, there is no place for practices that encourage corruption in this new world order.'

Aileen watched the seasoned councillors wince, a tiny smile playing on his lips. The use of Parshu-Raam's name was a clever touch. Over the past year, the son of Rishi Yamdagni had gone on a rampage, annihilating autocratic rulers from the Himalayas to the southern ocean, paving the way for a new and just class of kings. Brahmins, Vaishyas and Shudras were the new Kshatriyas of Nabhi-varsh and what remained of the old guard was still haunted by the prospect of Parshu-Raam's return. Aileen himself had been lucky to escape with his life. His superior, Kartavirya Arjun, the emperor of the world, had not been so fortunate.

Dushyant's closing argument had made even the most reluctant of councillors agree to the demand for modernization and as they passed a unanimous motion in favour of the idea, Aileen dismissed the court for the day and called his son to the throne.

'My son,' he said in a tone that betrayed his satisfaction, 'seeing the way you have convinced the senior councillors to change their stance for the benefit of the people, I am confident that you are quite ready to look after the affairs of this kingdom. Acharya Dirghatamas, other senior members of the family and I concur that the time has come to pass on the crown of Puruvansh.'

Kulguru Dirghatamas, a middle-aged rishi who stood behind the king, smiled in agreement.

Dushyant bowed to both the elders in gratitude and said, 'Father, it is only because of your blessings and the teachings of Gurudev that I stand where I am today.' Aileen had raised Dushyant and his brothers by himself in the absence of their mother who had died during childbirth. While the crown prince was glad he had been able to live up to his father's expectations, he was also concerned for his younger siblings and asked, 'What about my brothers, Father? May I be bold enough to suggest their induction into the royal council?'

The kulguru interrupted the conversation and said, 'Well, we can all agree that some of the councillors are living behind the times and need to be replaced with young blood. Dushyant's brothers are wise, well-versed in the principles of Dharma, and also love him deeply. They shall make capable and loyal ministers for our kingdom.'

Aileen was pleased with his son's generosity of spirit and the kulguru's sound advice; he gave a nod to the suggestion.

Taking an impromptu decision, he said to Dushyant, 'Why don't you and your brothers take a short retreat while the acharya checks for an auspicious muhurat to conduct the coronation ceremony? This may be the last time for all of you to relax before joining the court.'

The crown prince replied, 'Instead of spending this precious time on a holiday, I would like to utilize it in preparing for the responsibility that lies ahead. May I organize a hunting expedition instead?'

Aileen smiled again at the thoughtfulness of his son and gave his permission. Dushyant could have easily escaped to some exotic location in the Himalayas or taken a leisurely cruise on the Ganga with his brothers. Instead, he wanted to spend time in dense forests facing dangerous animals and chasing elusive prey. As he watched the retreating form of Dushyant with a satisfied look, the kulguru said, 'Rajan, I look forward to the future of our kingdom with immense hope.'

Aileen looked at him and asked, 'Gurudev, do you remember the time Parshu-Raam came to Hastinapur?'

Dirghatamas nodded, for that fateful day was indelibly etched in the memory of each citizen of Hastinapur. Even he, son of Devguru Brihaspati, had feared for his sovereign's life that day. The Brahmakshatriya had looked deep into Aileen's eyes, and after what had seemed like an interminably long moment, had blessed him with long life and prosperity. The entire council had breathed a sigh of relief. But then the Avatar had turned his gaze on the army generals and, in the blink of an eye, sliced through half of their ranks. Parshu-Raam had picked his way through the men with such speed and precision that by the time they could think of running to safety, he had already wiped out those harbouring Asurik tendencies.'

Shaking his head as if to clear it of the gruesome memories of that day, the king continued, 'I appreciate what the Avatar is doing and completely support his mission. But he filled my heart with serious doubts about the survival and future of our kingdom. Months after the onslaught, Hastinapur is still trying to get back on its feet. There are gaping holes in our ranks, and even those who have the capability to bear the responsibility are scared to step into the shoes of their predecessors.'

The acharya sympathized with the king. Refurbishing the depleted ranks of Hastinapur hadn't been easy. That is why it was important to change the rules and make more people eligible to participate in the running of the kingdom. The discussion that Dushyant had won today was a step in that direction.

'Don't worry, my king' he said, 'Dushyant, with his head full of fresh ideas, is perfectly capable of reviving Hastinapur's lost glory. His coronation shall bring forth a new wave of optimism and help the kingdom become greater than it ever has been before.'

The king nodded hopefully. 'I sincerely hope so, Gurudev. You've seen how the rajvaidya keeps hounding me to slow down and rest. Poor man! I know he worries about the state of my health. Even my family doesn't know about my failing heart. But my first responsibility is towards my kingdom; I won't be able to find peace until I see Dushyant sitting on the throne with my own eyes.'

'That day shall come soon enough, Rajan,' Dirghatamas said. 'We will need at least a fortnight to make all the arrangements, send invitations to the neighbouring kings making sure no one is left out, and prepare for their stay and comfort. Accordingly, I shall look for an auspicious muhurat towards the end of this month.'

Aileen waved his hand imperiously. 'Please do whatever needs to be done, Acharya. Just keep in mind I do not have long to live.'

The kulguru nodded and left the hall, summoning the royal attendants on his way out to take their sovereign to the royal chamber. Aileen was relieved to know he would be able to take the burden of running the kingdom off his shoulders soon. It was time for him to retire and let the next generation take charge.

Adhyaye 2

White snowy peaks towered over the lush green valley. A gurgling stream cut through pine and cypress forests, its waters cascading over rocks in waves of shimmering silver. It circled and meandered down the snowy slopes to nurture the wild cherry, apple and fig orchards that had been planted by the hermits living in the foothills of the mountains.

It was a beautiful morning and as Shakuntala stepped out of her austere hut, she could see the first yagnya fires going up to the heavens. The rising sun streamed through treetops, bathing the ashram in a golden glow. A light breeze carried on it the fragrance of the blue lotuses blooming in the shallow pool near the hermitage. Orange and black orioles flitted about in the foliage, chirping, while golden langurs chattered as they jumped from one branch to another, plucking horse chestnuts and mulberries. As their many sounds filled the ashram, Shakuntala smiled at the thought of their competing with the prayers of the faithful—both were thanking the gods in their own way.

Young hermits, dressed in coarse homespun jute, walked past her, bowing respectfully. She greeted them appropriately, moving towards the shrines along the perimeter to fulfil her daily ritual of honouring the gods who protected the hermitage. The first shrine was dedicated to Srishti-Karta Brahma, followed by one to Lord Shiva and then Shri Hari Vishnu. Other sanctums followed the standard template and were devoted to Indra, Surya, Chandra, Bhaag, Kuber, Dhata-Vidhata, Vayu and Varun.

That brought her to the shrine dedicated to Gayatri, the goddess of knowledge, first perceived by her birth father Brahmarishi Vishwamitra. She paused there for a moment, thinking about the man she had never met, yet knew everything about. He was the renowned Kshatriya king who had discovered the primeval Gayatri Mantra, and harnessed its power to become a Brahmarishi. The first human who had challenged the gods, spurned the affections of no less than an Apsara and forsaken all material attachments, including his own daughter. Last she heard, her birth father had taken up the post of kulguru in Ayodhya; she wondered how he was faring there.

The shrill call of a peacock pierced her reflections, bringing her back to the present. Banishing thoughts of Vishwamitra from her mind, she turned to look at the head of the ashram, the blessed soul who had more than made up for the absence of her birth parents—Maharishi Kanav.

The fair-complexioned septuagenarian was of average height and build, with genial features and a flowing beard that reached his midriff. His long grey hair was tied in a knot on top of his head and instead of the usual ochre or saffron robes of an ascetic he was dressed in white, the colour of purity. The Maharishi poured the final oblations in the sacrificial fire and rose to greet his adopted daughter. He was journeying into the hills to procure some herbs today and he wished to spend some time with her before he left.

As Shakuntala walked towards him, he noticed the heads of many young hermits turn to steal a glance at her. Even in the plain cotton sari she was wearing, her beauty was evident. Long raven hair framed a perfectly oval face and deep blue eyes that sparkled with innocence. Her alabaster complexion was so pure that it seemed even the slightest touch of dust would ruin its perfection, yet she walked through the rough earth and thorny shrubs as if she was born amongst them. He watched her with pride, thanking the gods for giving him such a beautiful and affectionate daughter.

Shakuntala greeted him with folded hands and asked, 'Father, may I have a word with you before you leave for the hills?'

As they walked away from the yagnya vedi, the Maharishi asked with concern, 'Is anything the matter, my dear? I hope my newly inducted students are not bothering you with their attentions.'

Shakuntala laughed at the suggestion. 'Not at all father, they are quite respectful, perhaps even a little afraid of approaching their guru's daughter. I just wished to make sure you don't forget to carry your own medicines while you explore the forests to find new ones for others!'

The Maharishi smiled and said with a slight bow of the head, 'What would I ever do without you, my child? I am so glad you chose to stay here rather than accompany your stepbrother Deval to Kanyakubja!'

Deval was the son and legal heir of Brahmarishi Vishwamitra and now ruled the kingdom of Mahodayapur from his palace in the capital, Kanyakubja. When he had found out about her existence, he had made all efforts to bring her back to the city but Shakuntala had refused. Not because she didn't appreciate

Deval's genuine brotherly concern but because she didn't want anyone to give her what was rightfully hers out of pity.

She responded to her father with a smile, 'Brother Deval has been very sweet in trying to compensate for our father's desertion, but nothing could ever persuade me to leave you behind in this ashram, alone!'

The venerable sage nodded and said, 'The day your blood relatives arrived from Kanyakubja, I felt so hopeless. You were the only ray of sunshine in my mundane life and, perhaps quite selfishly, I didn't want them to take you away. To their credit, they didn't force me in any way to relinquish you and I thanked the heavens when you refused to part from me. But Deval's suggestion of relocating the entire ashram was pure genius—this way he can stay in touch with you and you don't even have to leave your father alone.'

Shakuntala had learnt the real circumstances of her birth in childhood when the royal family of Kanyakubja had come calling at the Maharishi's ashram. They had graciously apologized for the burden the rearing of a young girl would have been on the Maharishi but he had reassured them that they had no cause to feel so for he doted on her. She had watched him talk to the strangers with a firmness that didn't brook further discussion and had loved him even more for it.

Had he wanted, Kanav could have let them take her away, getting rid of a responsibility he wasn't meant to shoulder. Instead, he had wrapped a protective arm around her and politely declined their offer. Years later Deval had come up with the idea of moving the whole ashram to Naimish Aranya, the forests at the border of Mahodayapur and Kosal, and they had relocated to the banks of the Malini river.

Shakuntala replied to her foster father's kind words with a smile, 'I suppose the fate gods do become generous sometimes! I just wish I had made some friends after we arrived here, then I wouldn't be so lonely all the time. Your students shy away from me as if I might eat them alive.'

The rishi laughed out loud and said, 'I promise to try and find someone capable of handling your fiery personality once I am back from the hills. But I do hope you won't leave my star pupils clutching a broken heart afterwards!'

Shakuntala chuckled at the thought and the entire ashram seemed to echo with the sound of tinkling bells. A few of the newly inducted Brahmacharis turned to look at her sun-lit face with longing and the fact didn't escape Kanav's notice. He dispassionately observed his daughter's ethereal beauty and knew it was cruel of him to subject the young celibates to such temptation.

Perhaps, more than a temporary companion, it was time to find a suitable match for his eligible daughter. It was time for him to stop being selfish and let her explore the possibilities that life had to offer.

Adhyaye 3

While Shakuntala was helping Maharishi Kanav pack for his journey, her birth father was about to send a Suryavanshi king packing in the neighbouring kingdom of Kosal.

Brahmarishi Vishwamitra stood in the royal hall facing King Harishchandra. With limbs as thick as tree trunks and a neatly trimmed beard on his handsome face, the kulguru of Ayodhya looked more like a warrior than a hermit. His tanned frame was draped in the ochre robes of a mendicant, his long dreadlocks were tied in a double knot on top of his head and he held a Brahma-dand in one of his hands.

The two men stood face-to-face, watched over by the massive granite statues of the twelve solar gods. The Brahmarishi's voice rang in the hall as he addressed the king imperiously, 'Harishchandra, I have served this kingdom as its chief-preceptor during a taxing period, saving not only your present life but also your afterlife from Yama's hell. It is only fair that I be paid as per my conditions.'

In his late thirties, the Suryavanshi king was tall and well-built with a healthy complexion and pleasant features, though at present his usually bright smile was replaced by an uncharacteristic frown. He replied in a confused tone,

'Gurudev, you undoubtedly saved me from Lord Parshu-Raam's axe and I have always been more than ready to repay that debt! Please tell me how I can be of service to you.'

Vishwamitra looked at the king haughtily and said with a smirk, 'You foolish man, saving you from my grand-nephew's wrath was my responsibility as the chief-preceptor of this kingdom. I do not wish any compensation for fulfilling what was my duty. You forget that even before Parshu-Raam started his mission, you had got yourself in a situation that would have doomed you for all eternity had I not come to your rescue.'

Harishchandra's face paled as he remembered the events that had led to Vishwamitra replacing Brahmarishi Vasishth as the kulguru of Suryavansh. In order to save his son's life, Harishchandra had pleaded with Vasishth to perform a procedure that reeked of dark magic. Vishwamitra, who had been passing through Ayodhya, had intervened in a way that allowed the terrible procedure to be completed without any blood being spilled. Vasishth had decided to go to the Himalayas to atone for his role in the event, leaving the kingdom in Vishwamitra's hands for the time being.

Trying to pacify the learned sage, he said, 'I am indeed indebted to you for saving me from an unimaginable sin that day and I cannot thank you enough for your intercession. Ask me anything, my lord, and I shall place it at your feet this instant!'

The Brahmarishi asked softly, 'What if I ask for something that you find impossible to donate, Harishchandra?'

The king was taken aback by the question but replied confidently, 'Barring the lives of my wife and son I can pledge anything for your happiness. I must make amends for compelling Brahmarishi Vasishth to perform dark magic; please help me get rid of this burden on my conscience.'

Vishwamitra looked at the king's face and nodded in satisfaction. 'So be it. Since you are so eager to please, I hereby demand this kingdom as payment of my services.'

The royal sabha erupted as the citizens protested at this unjust demand. The Brahmarishi stood with his back to the crowd, unaffected by the tumult while Harishchandra looked at his kulguru in surprise. Vishwamitra had earlier helped his father Satyavrat achieve his dream but for some strange reason was quite inimical to him. However, he was ready to go to any length to prove his genuine regret. Raising his hand to calm the crowd, he declared in a loud voice, 'From this very moment, I relinquish the right of kingship in favour of my mentor Brahmarishi Vishwamitra for as long as he chooses to rule over Kosal.'

Pandemonium broke out in the hall as people tried to make sense of what they had just heard. Some were rubbing their eyes, refusing to believe what they had witnessed, while others were crying against the harsh punishment being meted out to their king. For all his personal follies, Harishchandra was a just ruler and they couldn't understand how an interim kulguru could make the king abdicate his throne.

'Brothers and sisters of Ayodhya,' Harishchandra began solemnly as his preceptor left the assembly with a curt nod, 'please do not bear any ill will towards the learned guru. He does this for a reason.'

It took a moment for the enraged crowd to quiet down enough to be able to hear their king. Harishchandra's voice was full of conviction as he said, 'Not many of you remember that Lord Parshu-Raam had been a witness to the terrible deed

I had pushed Guru Vasishth to perform. Not only did I lose my self-respect that day, but I also lost our beloved kulguru who left us to atone for his actions.'

He let the significance of that sink in before adding, 'When the son of Rishi Yamdagni began destroying evil Kshatriyas, I was one of the first in his sights. He would have certainly taken my life had it not been for Brahmarishi Vishwamitra who assured him that I was a reformed man.'

There was pin-drop silence now. The crowd hung on his every word. Harishchandra sighed deeply and said, 'He may have done it to fulfil his duty as our kulguru, but Kosal still owes him for saving your king's life.'

The mood in the hall became sombre now as the realization dawned on the citizens that their king was looking for redemption. Harishchandra gauged the change in atmosphere and said, '*Suryavansh reet sada chali aayi, praan jayein par vachan na jayi*,' reminding them that a king of the solar dynasty could never go back on his promise.

'This ancient city's foundation was laid by the first man on earth, Manu himself, and anyone who sits on the Suryavanshi throne has to live up to its promise. I have pledged this hallowed throne to the Brahmarishi and intend to honour the debt we all owe him. He ruled Kanyakubja very ably for many years before becoming a Brahmarishi so I do not fear for the welfare of our kingdom. If he allows, I shall stay as a part of the council and help him take decisions for the continued welfare of Kosal.'

Folding his hands, he left the hall followed by the council members. They would need to sit together and discuss the implications of what had transpired in court that day.

Adhyaye 4

Going on a hunt was undoubtedly the most exciting sport for any Kshatriya. Raised on an invigorating routine of martial arts and physical workouts, most members of the warrior caste were quite enthusiastic about going into the forests for that was the closest they came to facing a real enemy during peacetime.

The forests of Nabhi-varsh abounded in wild game so the royal entourage was generally accompanied by a platoon of soldiers and hounds bred specifically for hunting. There were others who carried drums and cymbals to frighten the wild animals. The king typically rode trained elephants immune to both the noise as well as surprise attacks from overhanging branches.

However, Dushyant had wanted this to be a learning experience, a chance for him and his brothers to test their mettle against the wild beasts of the jungle. He had refused the paraphernalia, explaining to a worried Aileen that they would not be able to truly hone their reflexes from behind a curtain of protection. The brothers had headed deep into the jungle by themselves, while their personal guard followed at a discrete distance with specific orders not to intervene unless someone's life was in danger. They had set individual targets for each person and every day one of them would lead the attack, while the others supported him and watched his back. It was Dushyant's way of ensuring that all of them understood the importance of working together. The easiest animals to hunt were the deer, sambar and antelopes, but those were for the fat nobles, not sturdy young princes who had killed a fair number of wild boars by now.

It was the crown prince's turn to lead. They had entered the dense northern woods of Naimish Aranya that were home to leopards and other big cats. Soon after, Dushyant had spotted a panther perched on the sturdy branch of a blackberry tree and decided to pursue it. He shot a perfectly aimed arrow, but the graceful predator deftly dodged the projectile and sprang further into the dense forest. The princes had been tracking it for hours now, but were nowhere near locating the wily creature. Tired and exhausted, the small group halted at a spot dense with shisham trees.

Dushyant called out to his brothers, 'Shoor, Bhim, Pravasu, Vasu, this animal is proving to be quite elusive. Let's tarry a while and catch our breath before proceeding.'

His brothers agreed gratefully and dismounted from their steeds. As they sat down in the thicket, resting their weary limbs, Dushyant tied the horses around them in a circle and said, 'Stretch your legs while I keep watch. We shall rest for half a muhurat before picking up the trail again.'

'Brother,' the youngest Puru prince, Vasu, addressed him. 'It is my duty to take care of the elders, therefore allow me to keep watch in your stead.'

Dushyant smiled and shook his head, 'No, my dear boy, being the eldest, the responsibility to look after your safety is mine. Lie down, close your eyes and relax for some time. I'll wake you all once the sand has crossed the half mark,' he said pointing to the hourglass that hung from a satchel on his horse.

While his brothers slept, Dushyant decided to collect some dry branches to light a fire. The dense growth of trees blocked out most of the sunlight, rendering the forest quite cool. Midday had passed a muhurat back and the wind blowing from the northern mountains was adding to the slight chill. As Dushyant tried to light a fire by rubbing the dry sticks together, a sudden sound in the bushes alerted him to the presence of an animal. He leapt to his feet. The horses nickered nervously, but being well-trained for hunting parties, they did not react beyond that. Dushyant could sense their discomfort as he came closer to one of them and slowly looked around. What he saw stumped him completely. The panther they had been trying to track all this while was standing in a small clearing, staring right at him!

It stood majestically, looking in his direction with eyes that were like burning embers. Its magnificent body was about the length of two adult men and its spotted golden pelt camouflaged it well in the undergrowth. A frisson of excitement ran through Dushyant as he realized that the animal had cleverly reversed their roles, hunting its own hunters.

Aware that his short dagger would not be enough for an animal of such strength, he lunged to grab his spear. But the panther turned its back on him imperiously and sauntered off eastward. It stopped once to look back at him, as if daring him to follow its footsteps. Dushyant watched the retreating animal incredulously—this was the most bizarre behaviour he had ever seen in a wild animal!

His inquisitiveness got the better of him. Hastily grabbing his spear, he decided to follow the animal that was winding its way through the forest, through patches of light and darkness, gracefully leaping over fallen trees and anthills, unconcerned about being followed. It stopped at the entrance of what looked like a bamboo grove and then, with another glance at his pursuer, slid through the tall plants.

Following it at a safe distance, Dushyant entered the grove. A harem of peahens scattered noisily to protest his intrusion. Dushyant was startled at first but quickly getting his bearings, he looked around and noticed a remarkable change in flora. A gentle breeze, carrying on it the heady fragrance of wild flowers, caressed his weary face. To the tired and famished prince, it seemed like a veritable oasis.

'Where am I?' he wondered out loud, mesmerized by the surroundings. The panther had disappeared, but Dushyant no longer cared.

He could hear the sounds of a gurgling stream close by. A rainbow of flowers swung from the vines that were wrapped around mango trees. A few grapevines spread out in one corner, supported by short, stout sticks, and bees were hovering over them in an almost ecstatic frenzy. He plucked a few fruits and bit into them, their sweet nectar satisfying his parched throat, and thought of his brothers whom he had left sleeping. He had come so deep into the forest, that he didn't think he could find his way back, but he knew the guards were not too far behind and would find them soon enough.

As his gaze travelled over the grove, he was suddenly brought back to reality. For, there, sitting on the thick branch of a plum tree, looking straight at him with a decidedly human expression of contentment, was the panther that had led him here. Who was this creature who had truly and completely fooled him? His mind furiously worked out the different scenarios in which he could be ambushed.

Suddenly, he heard a human voice coming closer. Straining his ears, he took cautious steps towards it, keeping his spear ready for any eventuality. That was when the panther decided to make its move—and it didn't take Dushyant long to decide what to do. Clearly someone was in danger from the animal and as a Kshatriya it was his duty to save them. His spear poised to strike, he rushed out of the glen, and for the second time in that day, froze mid-action. In front of him, was the most beautiful girl he had ever seen in his life. And she was petting the wild animal as if it was a domestic cat!

'What are you doing?' the girl asked Dushyant in indignation. 'You are not allowed to bring arms in this sanctuary!'

Dushyant was flabbergasted. Instead of thanking him for trying to save her she was admonishing him for carrying a weapon! He struggled to explain his position. 'I was trying to save you from this panther, you silly girl! Who the hell are you and what are you doing in this forest?'

The girl did not take too kindly to the condescension in his tone and retorted, 'This panther belongs to this hermitage and never attacks humans. Who are *you* and what are you doing in our grove?'

'Well,' the prince said with barely restrained anger, 'I lost my way in the forest and was led to this grove by your beloved *pet* who, I daresay, has acted quite unlike any of his kind that I have seen in my kingdom.'

'*Your* kingdom?' she asked, surprised. 'This grove falls under the jurisdiction of Maharaj Deval of Kanyakubja. How and when did it become yours? The only other kingdom close by is that of Puru and last I heard, it was still ruled by Maharaj Aileen.'

Dushyant's face turned red with embarrassment as he confessed, 'I am still the king-in-waiting but shall be taking over the reins of the kingdom soon enough. I must have crossed into Mahodayan territory while following this curious animal!'

'You are Yuvraj Dushyant!' the girl exclaimed as realization dawned on her. Giving a short bow in recognition of his title she said in a conciliatory tone, 'Please excuse my rudeness. I should have thanked you for leaping to my rescue when you thought I was in distress. After all, you were unaware of the real nature of this gentle creature.'

Dushyant's bruised ego was massaged a little seeing the contrition on her face. 'I suppose that's all right.' Then his princely arrogance returned and he asked her, 'I still don't know who you are. What are you doing in the middle of the forest, and why do you own a panther?'

'I am the daughter of Brahmarishi Vishwamitra and the celestial Apsara Menaka. My mother left me in the forest after my birth and I was rescued by Maharishi Kanav who has raised me as his daughter. Maharaj Deval, king of Kanyakubja, is my stepbrother. It was he who set up this hermitage here. I came here looking for Badal, this panther that was missing since morning and . . .'

'And found me instead,' Dushyant finished with a cheeky smile. He vaguely remembered hearing about Vishwamitra from his kulguru, and of his dalliance with the celestial nymph. It was not surprising that this girl was born from an Apsara for no mortal woman could have given birth to such ethereal beauty. She was clearly not a child of this earth.

Shakuntala blushed at his statement but maintained her composure and asked politely, 'Would you care to come to our ashram? Dusk is fast approaching and I can send somebody to look for your group while you wash yourself and take some refreshments.'

Dushyant appreciated her concern. Her spirit did not seem to have been scarred by the events of her childhood. 'Maharishi Kanav has truly raised you well, my lady,' he replied in a softer tone. 'I accept your gracious offer till such time as my brothers can be notified.'

The sun had begun to set and he could hear the tinkling bells of the ashram cattle returning home. Shakuntala led the way towards her humble abode while the panther walked alongside, purring with satisfaction like a domestic cat. Dushyant silently thanked the animal for the part it had played in bringing him to this grove. He was a hopeful man; who knew where this chance encounter with this celestial beauty could lead.

Adhyaye 5

The news of her biological father's ascension to the throne of Ayodhya had reached Shakuntala through a travelling mendicant. The people of the Ashram were talking about how King Harishchandra had to atone for his actions, but she wondered if the fate gods would someday dare to punish Vishwamitra as well for abandoning her.

From the moment she had found out about her real parents, Shakuntala had found it difficult to avoid thinking about them. No matter how often she reminded herself that she had a really good life with Maharishi Kanav, her thoughts were plagued by the fact that neither of her birth parents had cared enough for her to raise her on their own. She had grown up surrounded by hermits of various orders and her birth father's spiritual achievements meant little to her. Whatever his professional accomplishments, he had still neglected the most important duty of a living being—that of looking after the children they had brought into the world and giving them the love and guidance they deserved.

Karma was capricious, you never knew when it would come back to reward you for an earlier good deed or punish you for an inadvertent transgression. What if destiny brought him back in front of her one day? How would she react? And what about her mother? Was she so lost in the revelries of Swarga that she had not found time to visit her daughter even once?

Shrugging their thoughts away had become a habit now and she did so again, focusing on the work at hand. In the absence of Maharishi Kanav, she had assumed responsibility of the royal guest, the crown prince of Hastinapur, for the past few days. Two young acolytes had been sent with refreshments for his brothers and a message from him. Dushyant did not want all of them to descend upon the ashram and disturb its harmony so he had asked them to head back to Hastinapur while he waited at the hermitage to seek the blessings of Maharishi Kanav before returning for his coronation.

There was another reason for his staying at the ashram. It was too early to confess but his heart had been stolen by this enchantress of the forest. Since his arrival, he had been trying to get to know Shakuntala better and whatever he had seen of her demeanour had only heightened his respect for her. He was trying different ways to impress her and was telling her about the lunar dynasty that he belonged to. 'The very birth of Chandravansh was a result of coming together of two different clans. Lord Chandra's son Budh married the granddaughter of Surya and their son Pururava managed to woo no less than Urvashi, one of the most ravishing Apsaras in Swarg.'

At that Shakuntala's thoughts went to her own mother who was believed to be the most beautiful Apsara in Indra's court. She wondered if Urvashi and her mother were friends and if so, whether she had advised Menaka against abandoning her family. Dushyant noticed the change in Shakuntala's expression and quickly steered the conversation in another direction, 'I am boring you with all this but I just wished to share with you the glorious history of Chandravansh.'

Shakuntala smiled and urged him to continue.

'Are you certain?' he asked, and at a nod from her, continued, 'Maharaj Pururava's grandson Nahush married Viraja from the clan of Pitris. Maharaj Yayati, the forefather of all Chandravanshi nations had two wives—one Brahmin and the other Daitya. Maharaj Prachinvat, who conquered the eastern nations, married a Naga princess. Closer home, my own great-grandfather Maharaj Matinar is believed to have sired children with Goddess Saraswati!'

'Saraswati, the river goddess?' Shakuntala asked incredulously.

'Yes,' Dushyant replied with pride, 'Maharaj Matinar performed a mammoth twelve-year yagnya on the banks of the river and, it is believed, at its successful completion, the goddess herself came before him and chose him as her husband. At least that's what I have been told by my grandfather.'

Shakuntala was too polite to give voice to her doubts. She herself was a child of a mortal and a nymph and was therefore in no position to judge another's fantastic stories. To put him at ease she asked in jest, 'So what exactly was the purpose of telling me all this, Yuvraj?'

Dushyant replied without missing a beat, 'I was hoping to impress upon you how unlike some other royal families, my clan has been open to the mixing of different gene pools since time immemorial. We Chandravanshis have a lot of freedom in choosing our life partners.'

Shakuntala's face turned crimson as she blushed at the implication. Living in the confines of the ashram, she had never encountered such a confident man and she was attracted to him in an inexplicable way. There was something in Dushyant's manner that made her want to know more about him but she could not let herself get carried away without hearing in words what he felt.

'And why would you want to impress me, Yuvraj?' she asked boldly.

'So that I can request you to become my wife and my queen,' came the reply. 'I have fallen head over heels in love with you, my lady!'

Shakuntala looked into his eyes appraisingly and a feeling of exhilaration ran down Dushyant's spine. He was a strong, virile, handsome man and a king-in-waiting, what else could a woman look for in a future husband? But her next words shook his self-confidence: 'You are perhaps grateful for the refuge I provided when you were lost in the forest. Or it could be that you have become infatuated with the beauty I inherited from my mother or, maybe, you are missing the damsels that fawn over you in the Puru court. Whatever the reason, Yuvraj, I find it hard to believe that you could have fallen in love with me in a matter of days,' Shakuntala chided.

Dushyant's face fell. She was right. How could she trust him, a stranger, with such an extreme claim? He himself hadn't thought about her in those terms consciously, but observing her ethereal beauty and caring nature over the past few days, the desire to have her in his life had become so intense that it had emboldened him to propose to her so audaciously.

He admired her forthrightness. 'You are right, my lady, it could be any of these reasons but believe me when I say it is not! Only a blind man would be immune to your beauty and charm, but that is not what has captivated my heart. I have watched you manage the ashram in the absence of the Maharishi with aplomb. I have witnessed how you mingle with the old and the young with equal warmth and seen you tend to the animals and plants diligently every day. I have seen you the way you *are*, my lady. Trust me, it is not just your outer appearance that has stolen my heart but your inner beauty as well.'

Shakuntala was surprised to learn that he had noticed her entire routine without her being aware of it. The knowledge gave her a strange sense of accomplishment and filled her heart with a warmth she hadn't felt before. This was a new feeling, the feeling of being liked by someone for who *she* was, and not her family, parentage or social status. She had to admit that it was a decent proposal—a bit sudden, yes—but definitely worth considering. There was no doubt that Dushyant was very good-looking. He had the courteous and pleasant manner of a man who had been bred in nobility. Besides, the prospect of improving her social status that this alliance provided appealed to her as well. She was the daughter of a Chandravanshi and Dushyant belonged to the lunar dynasty as well. He could give her the position she would have been entitled to had she not been forsaken by her father. Now she could become a queen without taking help from either her birth father in Ayodhya or her stepbrother in Kanyakubja and the possibility thrilled her.

Dushyant saw her vacillate and knew he had to take one final chance. He grasped her hands in his and whispered softly, 'My feelings for you are true and they remain unchanged even after your rebuke. Isn't that proof enough of the genuineness of my affection?'

Shakuntala's resolve was beginning to waver and Dushyant saw that in her face. He pulled her to him, his masculine fragrance suffusing her senses. She looked at him in silence, her lotus eyes filled with a longing that dared him to do the unthinkable. Desire bloomed between them, filling them with anticipation. He knew now that she wanted him. Hoping to remove any remaining doubts in her mind, he said, 'The denizens of forests do not follow the rules of the cities and do not require permission from anyone before choosing their mate. The validity of such a marriage, the Gandharv Vivah, is upheld even by the Dharma Shastras. Still, if that doesn't convince you, I promise to take your father's permission too as soon as he is back in the hermitage.'

Shakuntala replied in a soft voice, 'I know the laws of the Gandharvs, Yuvraj, but I am not one of them.'

'Yes, but you *do* live in the forest,' Dushyant countered, 'and you are equally free to choose your husband. I promise you that I will never let you down nor will I allow anyone to question the sanctity of our relationship.'

Shakuntala's mind was in turmoil; how could she take the plunge into marital life without her adoptive father's consent? Her head was warning her against going ahead with a ceremony that would mean little without the presence of witnesses, but for the first time in her youthful life, desire had gripped her heart. She thought of her parents who had lived together without anyone's approval; life seemed to have come full circle as she contemplated doing the same herself. But she could not let her own offspring suffer the ignominy that she had endured.

Choosing her words carefully she said, 'I shall take your hand in mine on one condition. Promise me that if this union results in a child, he or she shall become the heir to the throne of Hastinapur!'

Upon hearing her condition, the respect Dushyant had for her grew even more. She could have just lived in the moment, satisfying her own desires, but even now her heart cared more for those yet to come into this world. He looked into her eyes and said with all the conviction that he could muster, 'I hereby promise that you shall be my only queen and your child will sit on the moon throne of Hastinapur after I retire.'

Shakuntala sat down with relief when she heard those words. She had never taken such an important decision on the spur of the moment. But Dushyant's presence was filling her with a heady feeling of hope and the exhilaration of newfound love. The prince hastily plucked a nearby vine and knotted its ends together to create a makeshift garland. He placed it around Shakuntala's neck with a feeling of elation while she took off the string of lotus flowers tied around her mid-riff and placed it on his strong shoulders.

The instant the simple ceremony got over, Dushyant clasped her in his arms. An unknown thrill ran down Shakuntala's body. She was about to plunge into the forbidden and was no longer responsible for what happened hereafter. As he pressed his lips to hers, she finally understood the ecstasy of consummation that had brought her parents together. Her entire frame trembled with desire. Dushyant too was carried away on a tide of longing. She seemed to fuse into his very bones, her existence coursing through his veins like a hypnotic elixir.

Shakuntala gloried in this new sensation, the deliciousness of losing herself to her prince. She was no longer a girl abandoned in the forest and raised by an old rishi in a far-off hermitage; she was a woman now, loved by the man who would be the king of an ancient Chandravanshi kingdom. Her destiny was finally changing and she would make the most of the opportunity it had provided.

Adhyaye 6

While the fate gods seemed to be smiling upon Shakuntala at last, her father was enjoying wiping the smile off the face of his erstwhile king.

The first family of Ayodhya had been asked to vacate the palace. Harishchandra now stood in the nave of the royal hall like a commoner along with his wife, Taramati, and son, Rohitashwa. The Brahmarishi was talking to them in a voice dripping with condescension, 'Harishchandra, you have abdicated the throne to repay the debt you owed me. But I have realized something that had escaped my notice earlier.'

'What else can I do for you, my lord?' the Suryavanshi asked with all humility.

Vishwamitra broke into a sardonic smile as he said, 'Even though you have repaid the debt satisfactorily, the interest on it still remains.'

Harishchandra looked at his erstwhile guru in bewilderment.

Vishwamitra explained, 'The debt that you settled with your kingdom was owed for a long time. I couldn't collect it earlier because of the unceremonious arrival of my grand-nephew, Raam. There is, however, the small matter of the interest that is due for the entire duration of delay.'

Every eye in the hall turned towards their new king with hostility; Vishwamitra was exacting an unusual revenge on Harishchandra and the people of Ayodhya refused to let him further humiliate their beloved king. The leader of the royal council had a hurried discussion with his colleagues and stood up to declare, 'The royal council of Ayodhya is ready to pay any amount that the learned guru deems fit as payback for the inadvertent delay in repaying our king's debt.'

Harishchandra's heart melted seeing the loyalty of his ministers.

The Brahmarishi, on the other hand, seemed to perceive it as an affront to his authority. 'Harishchandra is no longer the king of Ayodhya,' he said with a contemptuous look, 'and the council would do well to remember that. The debt and its interest are owed by the son of Satyavrat, the man for whom I once challenged Indra himself! I protected Harishchandra from the wrath of Parshu-Raam and entreated Varun, the lord of the oceans, to save the life of his only son. Surely your "king" can pay a small interest for services rendered to three generations of his family without burdening the kingdom of Kosal?'

Harishchandra raised his hands to quieten the occupants of the hall and addressed the Brahmarishi in a placatory tone, 'Pardon them, my lord, for they speak out of their love for me. I shall be more than happy to proffer the interest that you desire and rightfully deserve. Pray tell me, what is it that you wish for?'

'Your time to grant wishes is over, Harishchandra,' Vishwamitra drawled in the same bored tone. 'You have already relinquished control of the throne and the riches of Kosal that come with it. How do you intend to pay me now?'

The truth of these words hit Harishchandra. The Brahmarishi was right. He did not possess anything, save the clothes on his back. Thinking of a way out, he said, 'My lord, like a true guru, you show me the path even in your censure. I do not own anything now but I *can* find a way to earn a living. If you give me a month's time, I promise to find employment and pay back the amount due to you.'

The Brahmarishi considered Harishchandra's request, and then nodded. 'That sounds like a reasonable arrangement. I give you a month's time to repay the interest owed to me which I am fixing at three hundred gold coins,' he declared magnanimously. 'But, I have one condition.'

The entire hall waited with bated breath as Vishwamitra uttered his next words. 'If you stay in Ayodhya, your citizens shall help you collect the money in no time. I want you to leave Kosal, cross the Naimish Aranya and go to Kanyakubja, the capital of my erstwhile kingdom, to earn your living. I shall add two more weeks to account for your travel there and back, but at the end of these six weeks, I want all my dues settled.'

Harishchandra knew the Brahmarishi was deliberately making the conditions harder for him but he accepted his condition gracefully.

Vishwamitra then pointed to his family and said, 'A man's kin are his own responsibility. The kingdom of Kosal cannot accept the burden of looking after them in your absence. You will have to take them with you when you leave Ayodhya.'

The courtiers in the assembly rose up in protest and this time even Harishchandra could not stop himself from retorting, 'Gurudev, this is an extremely unjust demand! My wife and son have nothing to do with my debts and I do not wish to jeopardize their future because of my past mistakes.'

Vishwamitra rose from the throne in a huff. 'Enough! The will of the king is the will of God! I shall not tolerate any more insubordination in this court.' The hall fell silent. 'Do not forget, Harishchandra,' he continued, 'that the abominable procedure you forced Brahmarishi Vasishth to perform was done for the sake of this very son. Both you and your wife thought nothing of sacrificing an innocent Brahmin boy to save the life of your own child; she is as much a part of this sin as you. It is only fair that the punishment for this be distributed amongst the three of you as well.'

He glared at the citizens and declared, 'As my first imperial decree, I hereby exile Suryavanshi Harishchandra, his wife, the erstwhile queen Taramati, and their son, Rohitashwa, from the kingdom of Kosal. They shall be allowed entry into Ayodhya at the end of six weeks, subject to their fulfilling all my conditions!'

Harishchandra hung his head in resignation. Folding his hands, he turned his back on the throne he had once given royal orders from himself. The councillors in their high seats watched him walk out with his family but none dared intercede on his behalf now. The twelve granite gods adorning the hall seemed to commiserate with him, but could do little. A hopeless despondence engulfed Harishchandra, but inside him a resolve was strengthening. He would not let his wife and their cherished son face any troubles on his account. He was the head of their family, and king of Ayodhya or not, he could still earn a livelihood for them.

Adhyaye 7

Dushyant had taken the biggest decision of his life without consulting anyone in his family and as much as he would have liked to, he could not wait for the Maharishi any more.

As he got ready to mount the ashram steed that would take him to Hastinapur, he said to Shakuntala with genuine regret, 'I feel like Satyavrat, the Suryavanshi king whom your father saved from spending eternity dangling between the heavens and earth. My heart is split in two for I cannot bear to leave you but I must go to Hastinapur to seek my father's permission to bring you home.'

Shakuntala too was deeply affected by his departure but did not let it show lest it weaken his resolve. Reassuring him, she said, 'Please do not fret over me. I am well aware of the enormity of the task in front of you. I have to break the news to my father as well and I can only hope he is as accepting of our union as you claim the Chandravanshis are.'

Dushyant moaned in complaint, 'O Shakuntala! How will I ever bear this separation! Know that what departs from this grove is just my body; my heart I leave behind with you. My spirit shall remain here, protecting you from the bees when you water your plants, caressing your silken tresses as you tend to your pets, holding you in an embrace when you fall asleep at night—'

'Don't say such things,' Shakuntala said mournfully, 'I will never be able to do any of this without thinking of you now!'

Dushyant held her close and whispered, 'Be brave, my love, and wait for the day when I return for you, leading a procession of elephants, horses and gold palanquins.' As an afterthought he added, 'If because of the formalities related to the coronation I cannot come myself, and have to send for you, please do not think I have deserted you!'

Shakuntala laughed at the thought but then saw that Dushyant was serious. She watched as he took off his ring and placed it in her palm.

'This ring has Hastinapur's insignia and my name engraved on it. It shall be your proof in case someone is so blind as to not recognize your beauty from my description. Read one letter of my name every day and even before you reach the end, my men will have come to bring you to our palace.'

Shakuntala realized the practicality of the gesture and took the ring. 'I hope I can see you become the king of Hastinapur with my own eyes.'

'You shall, my love,' vowed Dushyant, 'I will not wear the crown without my queen by my side.'

With these parting words, he mounted the stallion to begin his journey to the Puru capital. Shakuntala returned to the ashram, her heart feeling heavier than lead. When Badal, the panther that had brought Dushyant to her all those days ago, nudged her hand she burst into tears, hugging its neck. Her condition hadn't gone unnoticed by the other residents of the hermitage and a few older women came to console her. They had refrained from interfering in her life since it was not their place to chaperone her in the absence of her father, but they comforted her now and asked her to speak to her father as soon as he was back.

As luck would have it, Maharishi Kanav returned to the ashram the same evening with baskets full of rare herbs. Giving directions to the students who had accompanied him to store things in their proper places, he went to meet his daughter. The moment he stepped into her hut, he could sense the change in atmosphere. Shakuntala was sitting in a corner, completely oblivious to his arrival, which was unusual for she was always the first to greet him after every expedition.

He called out to her softly, 'How are you, my child?'

Shakuntala looked up with a start and rushed to touch his feet. 'Father!' she exclaimed. 'When did you arrive? I am sorry I didn't even realize you had returned!'

'It's understandable,' Kanav said with a smile. 'After all, one can only think of one person at a time.'

Shakuntala heaved a sigh of relief as she realized that the maharishi had used his yogic powers to divine the reason for her despondence. It saved her from the awkwardness of revealing the events of the past few days, though she was afraid he might be upset with her for taking such a big decision herself.

The maharishi saw the look on her face and said supportively, 'Don't worry, my child. We are not living in a Suryavanshi kingdom where women are bound by the strict laws laid down by Manu. Even if we were, the laws of the cities do not apply to the hermits living in forests. Your union with the Chandravanshi crown prince has my complete approval.'

Shakuntala gasped with happiness and embraced her adoptive father as he continued, 'Truth be told, living here in the forest, I couldn't have found a better husband than Dushyant for you. From what I know of his family, his father, Maharaj Aileen, was one of the few Kshatriyas left untouched by Parshu-Raam when he went on a rampage. That itself says a lot about the worthiness of their dynasty.'

The old rishi patted her head affectionately and asked her to start packing to attend her husband's coronation. Having put her fears to rest, he stepped out to give some more thought to the events that had occurred in his absence. While he wholeheartedly supported Shakuntala's choice, he understood the frailties of the human mind all too well. Dushyant was a virile young man with raging hormones. Would his dalliance with Shakuntala amount to anything more than a fling? He had promised Shakuntala that he would make her his queen, but would he keep his word now that he had parted from her? Besides, now that he was to be crowned monarch, Hastinapur was sure to be inundated with numerous marriage proposals for daughters of various other kings. He thought of the multiple possibilities that could ruin his daughter's dreams and sighed.

If only things in this world could happen the way the young envisioned them . . .

Adhyaye 8

Harishchandra and his family reached Kanyakubja after a full week and were awestruck by the temples, palaces, community halls, public baths, granaries, amphitheatres and fragrant gardens gracing various parts of the city. Mahodayapur had become the most prosperous kingdom in Nabhi-varsh under Vishwamitra's rule, and there were telltale signs everywhere. Harishchandra was sure he would be able to earn well here but whether it would be sufficient to repay the Brahmarishi remained to be seen. While leaving Ayodhya, they had been allowed to carry only what they had been wearing. Harishchandra had used his personal jewels to procure food and transport for the journey. Taramati offered her own ornaments to secure accommodation for a month at a traveller's inn, and he had no choice but to accept. He was heartbroken to see his beloved wife and son suffering, but it also strengthened his resolve to set things right as soon as possible.

There were many artisans' guilds in the city—he could work for one of them. Making up his mind, he headed to the central market, intending to auction himself to the highest bidder. Perhaps someone would be foolhardy enough to hire

41

him and give him the amount he so desperately needed. At the market square, he gathered courage to address the inhabitants of the city that had once been ruled by the very man who had put him in this condition. Clearing his throat, he proclaimed in a loud voice, 'Good citizens of Kanyakubja, a newcomer to your city requests your indulgence for a moment.'

His regal bearing and commanding voice caught the attention of a few passers-by but only momentarily. He tried again. 'I do not have any goods to sell but I can offer the services of a hard-working man. I am strong and eager to learn any trade that will allow me to earn three hundred gold coins in one month.'

A few of those who had gathered around him burst out laughing. One of the traders mocked his tone and said, 'Three hundred coins for someone who doesn't have anything to offer save himself? You must be *really* new in this city!'

This was the first time someone had ridiculed Harishchandra. The reality that he was no longer a king hit him hard. There was another round of guffaws and then a female trader asked him, 'Why would anyone pay that much to an unskilled person when one can get a good apprentice for one-fifth of that amount?'

In all his years, the Suryavanshi had never lacked the skills required for any task he had to accomplish, but the woman was right—what could he offer them? This was a new experience for him. Swallowing his pride, he said, 'I agree my price is a little high for the market, but it's not every day that you get the chance to hire a former king as your helper!'

The statement was greeted with another round of raucous laughter. One trader remarked, 'A king who doesn't have a kingdom? Are you one of those who hid behind their women to save their lives when Parshu-Raam came to deliver justice? What are they called . . . Ah, yes, I remember. A Nari-kavach!'

The taunt was made in jest but Harishchandra felt the jibe deep in his heart. He was no coward and had not sought shelter with any woman to save his life, but the bitter truth remained that he had been saved only because of Vishwamitra's intervention. Perhaps it would be best if he did not mention his true identity again.

'No, my friend,' he said in as jovial a tone as he could muster, 'I am but a common man who once ruled the hearts of many people in another kingdom. Circumstances have brought me to your gracious city and I hope you shall give me an opportunity to earn the same good fortune.'

When he did not receive any encouraging responses, he began to despair. Raising his voice one last time he asked, 'Good citizens of Kanyakubja, is there no one who can give work to a man on faith? I am willing to do absolutely anything to raise the money. I implore you! Help me for the sake of my wife and son.'

His words rang true but nobody was willing to take a risk on someone they didn't know. Had he been a resident of their city they could have verified his antecedents and perhaps someone might have employed him, but that was impossible. Just when Harishchandra was about to give up, a deep voice was heard.

'I will take a chance on you.'

Harishchandra looked expectantly in the direction the voice had come from but his face fell as soon as he saw the person it belonged to—it was a chandal, a keeper of the crematorium. He was a tall man with matted hair and a scraggy, grey beard and moustache. His clothes were coarse and unkempt and judging by the reaction of those standing next to him, he probably hadn't bathed in a long time. He was flanked by a couple of dogs who looked just as dishevelled as their master.

Harishchandra knew this man would not have the kind of money he required, yet he couldn't possibly refuse outright the only offer he had received. Choosing his words carefully, he replied politely, 'Honoured sir, I am thankful for your gracious offer but the amount I need is significant. I require three hundred gold coins and I am afraid I may not be able to earn that much working in the crematorium.'

'I will give you three hundred coins,' said the man imperiously. At that, the people around them turned to gawk at him. He found his own scepticism growing as he looked at the citizens who were watching them in disbelief. Many couldn't believe that the caretaker of a crematorium had that kind of money to offer. 'I am no ordinary chandal, but the caretaker of the largest crematorium in this part of Nabhi-varsh. If you are too proud to accept the only offer you have, maybe you really do not deserve being given a chance by Veerbahu.'

As he made to turn, Harishchandra stopped him with a plea. 'Pardon my incredulity, sir, and take me with you! I am ready to go to the ends of the earth to repay my debt.'

'You needn't go that far,' Veerbahu responded. 'The crematorium is at the edge of the city.' He glanced contemptuously at the people staring at them. 'No one can avoid coming to my workplace forever. The crematorium is the final resting place of all men and women, even you who stand here, making faces. This man has just managed to arrive a little earlier than you, but make no mistake, I shall see each one of you sooner or later.'

Some of the superstitious ones gasped at his prediction and hurried away while others dismissed him as a madman. Even Harishchandra felt the dread of his words and shuddered imperceptibly. Steeling his resolve, he said, 'I don't care what anyone thinks, my lord. Please tell me when and where to begin work.'

Veerbahu looked at him with renewed interest and said, 'You may not be such a bad apprentice after all. But I have one condition—you have to sever all ties with this city of hypocrites for as long as you are working for me.'

The Suryavanshi was mystified by the strange man as well as his offer but he could not let this opportunity pass. Nodding in agreement, he said, 'I shall not fail you! Please permit me to go home and inform my family. I shall come to you right after that.'

The man turned around with his dogs and Harishchandra ran to the inn, bursting with excitement. Taramati's fair face lit up when he told her the news but the next instant she balked at the idea of his toiling in a crematorium. She refused to let him work in the resting place of the dead and offered him an alternative, 'Why don't we sell our remaining jewels to cover some part of our debt? You can then look for a better place to work at even if it means earning a little less money!'

Harishchandra shook his head and said, 'You will need those to procure food and other necessities in my absence. The Brahmarishi shrewdly demanded that we take only what we had on us at the time, thereby limiting our access to even our own personal collections. Moreover, I cannot in all good conscience repay him with money that I haven't *earned* myself!'

Taramati's face fell hearing the resolve in her husband's voice. Seeing her crestfallen expression, Harishchandra ended the conversation by saying, 'Stop worrying! Nothing will happen to me. We must do whatever is required to repay our debt to Brahmarishi Vishwamitra and no ghosts or goblins can shake my resolve. You just take care of yourself and our son. I shall see you after a month.'

Adhyaye 9

The royal hall of Hastinapur was enveloped in an unnatural silence, punctuated by an occasional sound of anguish as the citizens of Puru paid their respects to their deceased king.

Dushyant had started for home, bursting with excitement, but things had changed on the way. He was intercepted by messengers from the palace who told him that his father, Maharaj Aileen, had succumbed to a massive heart attack three nights before. The Puru capital was drowning in sorrow and as he entered the royal hall to see his father for the last time, Dushyant's eyes filled with tears. The exquisite sandalwood moon throne stood vacant, as if it too mourned the passing of its most recent occupant. Aileen's body was placed in a silver casket that had been filled with sesame oil to preserve it till his son's return. To Dushyant, his father appeared to be sleeping peacefully, but this was a sleep he would never wake from. His siblings came forward and Dushyant let himself be embraced by them as they all silently grieved.

The kulguru, who had begun making arrangements for the cremation as soon as Dushyant had arrived, addressed the brothers now, 'We have to say goodbye to Maharaj soon. His life force has left but we still need to return his mortal body to the five elements with due ceremony.'

The guru's voice soothed Dushyant's grief-stricken mind for the time being and he tried to focus on what was required of him. The Antim Sanskar or last rite did little for the departed soul but was important to provide closure to the devastated family. The king's lifeless body was carried to the cremation ground on the shoulders of his five sons while other family members and guests followed behind. The path to the crematorium was lined with grieving citizens who showered flower petals as their king took his last journey through the city. Aileen had cared for his subjects like his own children and not only the citizens but also neighbouring kings had come to pay their last respects and offer condolences.

At the crematorium, Dirghatamas directed them to place the body on a sandalwood pyre. Once the king had been laid to rest for the last time, he pointed to an earthen pot with a hole on one side and instructed Dushyant to hold it on his left shoulder. 'As the eldest son of Maharaj Aileen, you shall perform the entire ceremony. Walk around the pyre in an anti-clockwise direction with the pot on your shoulder, making sure that all the water has been used up by the time you complete the circle.'

When Dushyant had followed his instructions, the kulguru asked him to throw the pot behind him over his shoulder without turning around. The prince understood that the act had both scientific and symbolic value—the line of water created a protective boundary for the wood that would soon be lit while the breaking of the empty pot signified the breaking of all bonds between the living and the deceased.

Acharya Dirghatamas then asked him to place grains of rice in his father's mouth and sprinkle ghee on the body. This would help mask the smell of burning flesh once it had been lit. Agni, the fire god, was believed to take the soul of the deceased to the land of the forefathers. Under the guru's guidance, Dushyant took up the ceremonial torch and finally lit the pyre, repeating the guru's words:

'Burn him up, but do not consume him, Agni, let not his
    body be scattered without use,
When you have matured him and made ready for the
    new life,
Send him over to the land of the forefathers,
Help him follow the will of the gods, and may his merit
    take him to the heavens.'

Once the pyre was ablaze, prayers were recited to the deities to help the departing soul reach the world of the pitris. When the last rites were over, Dushyant waited for everyone to leave, wanting to grieve in solitude. His brothers tried to persuade him to return with them but he didn't budge. Once his family had left, he fell down on the soft sand around the pyre, staring at the burning embers with eyes full of pain and regret. The day had passed by in a blur, his guilt for not being there for his father accentuating his grief. His entire body was racked with powerful sobs as he gave vent to the remorse that weighed on his spirit.

He felt a hand caress his head and turned his face to see the shadowy form of Acharya Dirghatamas. The guru's gaunt frame was wrapped in a white robe and his sagacious look was heightened by his own grief. Dushyant and his brothers had been tutored by the kulguru from childhood and he clung to his guru's feet now, weeping piteously.

'It is all right, my son,' the guru said in a sombre tone. He understood how the prince felt about his absence at the time of his father's death and tried to comfort him. 'You can't blame yourself for not being here when Maharaj passed away. No one other than the rajvaidya knew about the king's heart condition and even he was surprised by the severity of the attack.'

Dushyant's mind registered surprise for this was the first he was hearing of his father's ailment. Even though he acknowledged the fact that he couldn't have done anything had he been in Hastinapur he could not shake the feeling that it was somehow his responsibility.

'How can I not blame myself, Gurudev?' he asked in an anguished voice. 'I was supposed to return four days ago, yet I extended my stay in the forest. Do you know the reason? I was satiating my lust in the arms of a woman I had just met, while my father was in his death throes. I will never forgive myself for this indiscretion!'

The kulguru was taken aback by the prince's confession but thought it wise not to interrupt him as he poured his heart out. 'How could I have been so selfish?' Dushyant said between sobs. 'Had I not succumbed to my lust I would have been in Hastinapur days ago; perhaps I could have helped father in some way. At least he would have had the satisfaction of looking at the faces of all his sons in his last moments! And what of me, Gurudev? I did not even get to bid farewell to him.'

Dirghatamas gently stroked his head and said, 'Yuvraj, you have to forget what happened in the forest. Youth brings with it its fair share of mistakes and you cannot dwell on them if you wish to move ahead in life. With the passing of your father, the responsibility of the kingdom falls on your shoulders. Maharaj Aileen had wished to crown you as soon as you returned from the hunt and it is imperative that we fulfil his last wish as soon as possible.'

Dushyant stopped sobbing and looked at the kulguru with swollen eyes. 'I shall do everything that is required of me, Gurudev. Please guide me and show me the right path,' he said with folded hands.

Dirghatamas knew he had to get Dushyant ready to face the huge task that lay ahead of him. He said in a comforting voice, 'You are ready for this responsibility, my prince. It is only when a king fears nothing and wishes for nothing that he can discharge his duties towards his kingdom appropriately. The coronation shall be held tomorrow morning so that all the relatives and friends who came for Maharaj's funeral can be a part of it.'

Dushyant nodded and let the guru lead him back to the palace. His infatuation with Shakuntala had kept him away from his own father at the time of his death. He would never make the mistake of meeting the half-Apsara again. With the remorse in his heart overshadowing the memories of his association with her, he resolved to forget the promises he had made in the forest. Shakuntala could not become a part of his life.

Adhyaye 10

Dawn was yet to break on the eastern horizon but she was already wide awake. It was becoming a habit now. Lately she had begun finding it difficult to even fall asleep and would often spend the entire night tossing and turning in bed. When she did manage to sleep, thoughts of him would overwhelm her like a tidal wave, setting her adrift on a hopeless quest.

It had been one month since Dushyant had left; one whole month that she hadn't heard from him. Shakuntala had been elated by her father's acceptance of their relationship and had immediately started preparing for the imminent journey but the royal summons from Hastinapur never arrived. She knew Dushyant's messengers would take a few days to reach her, but then the days had turned into weeks and her understanding had given way to anxiety.

She rose from the bed and started pacing the room. It was too dark to go out so she had to stay in the small hut no matter how oppressive it felt. Over the past weeks her face had lost its glow and dark circles had appeared under her eyes. Her usual exuberance was gone and she went about her daily chores indifferently, sometimes barely finishing them. Even the plants and animals of the ashram were beginning to look listless in her neglect.

Her heartbeat quickened and hope flared whenever she heard footsteps approaching, only to be brutally dashed again. She knew the residents of the hermitage were talking about her situation though they were kind enough not to say anything to her face. But everyone, including her father, had the same question on their minds: Would Dushyant ever call her to Hastinapur?

She was still pacing when a sudden gust of wind blew out the solitary lamp in the hut, plunging it into an inky darkness. She heard the door to her hut open. Who could be entering her hut at this hour? For a moment she imagined that Dushyant had come to whisk her away in some perverse romantic fashion. But then her mind told her not to be overly optimistic.

Unable to see anyone in the darkness, she called out in a troubled voice, 'Who's there?'

A shadowy figure stood in the doorway, silhouetted against the meagre light of torches outside. As the figure stepped inside, she realized it wasn't a man.

'Who is it?' she asked again, this time in anger, wondering if she should shout for help.

As if in response, an ethereal glow began illuminating the figure and the door shut of its own accord. Shakuntala had heard of forest spirits and Yakshas and wondered if one of those semi-divine beings had decided to pay her a visit. She watched, mesmerized by the spectre, and as the soft glow reached the face of the mysterious visitor, she gasped in surprise—it was her own face looking at her!

Was she dreaming, she wondered. Perhaps she had died of heartbreak in her sleep and was now looking at her own soul come to bid her goodbye? She rubbed her eyes and pinched herself twice but the vision was still there. She was definitely looking at her lookalike but the woman in front of her was dressed in finery that she neither possessed nor had ever dreamt of in her life.

'How are you, Daughter?' the vision addressed her in a soft, lilting voice.

As the words registered in Shakuntala's mind, realization struck her like lightening and she reeled in shock. Breathing hard, she leaned against the wall for support. The apparition, her doppelganger, was the most famous Apsara from Indra's court, her mother, Menaka!

'How are you, my child?' Menaka asked again but Shakuntala was at a complete loss for words.

What could she say to the mother who had abandoned her at the very moment of her birth? As the Apsara took a step towards her, Shakuntala finally blurted in anger, 'Don't call me that! I am an orphan raised by Maharishi Kanav. He is the only parent I have!'

Once her initial shock had subsided, she looked at the celestial being critically. Her birth mother was tall and voluptuous, her diaphanous sari clinging to every curve of her body. Her long, lustrous dark hair was tied in a braid that extended to her hips. Strings of pearls adorned her head, neck and midriff while other precious stones glittered on her wrists and fingers. Her face seemed to be made of molten gold, with hints of peach and rose thrown in, and her kohl-lined eyes were the colour of brilliant sapphires.

'Shakuntala, listen to me,' Menaka said and advanced a few steps but her daughter retreated to the farthest corner of the small hut.

'What do you want from me?' Shakuntala asked in anguish. 'Why are you tormenting me at a time when I am already in deep trouble?'

'That is precisely why I have come to you, my child,' Menaka said in a soft voice, 'I can't bear to see you go through the same agony that I experienced while carrying you! All your life, there has been someone to look after you, but there is no one who can share the sorrow of your heart right now.'

'And you think I will share it with you? Who are you to come barging into my life after two decades of neglecting me?' Shakuntala asked in disbelief. She was at a loss for how to deal with her mother and sat down by the wall away from her.

A change came over the Apsara's features and her eyes welled up with tears. Menaka addressed her in a choked voice, 'I know you won't believe me but leaving you was not easy for me at all! You are my firstborn and perhaps the only child I will ever have in my life. Even the most cold-hearted mother wouldn't leave her first child.'

'Yet you did,' Shakuntala said scornfully. 'Says a lot about you, doesn't it, *Mother*?'

Menaka's body slumped to the floor and tears flowed from her eyes. She took some time to compose herself and said, 'You can judge me all you want but you do not know the circumstances in which I left you. I was sent by Indra to disrupt your father's penance and following his instructions was my duty. However, I had failed to consider my own feelings and for the first time in my life, I, the seductress of Swarg, lost my heart to someone.'

In spite of her reluctance, Shakuntala found herself wanting to know more about what had transpired between her parents. She had always assumed that theirs was a passing affair but her mother's words seemed to suggest otherwise.

'Your father and I stayed together for ten years,' Menaka said, 'and each day was more precious to me than a year spent in heaven. I was ready to forsake my immortality for him, Shakuntala. Can you imagine what that means to a celestial being?'

Shakuntala looked at her quietly, beginning to comprehend that things may not have been as easy for her mother as she had imagined.

The nymph continued, 'You may not know it, but unlike mortals, Apsaras can control their bodily functions. Letting you take root in my womb was a conscious decision that I took to strengthen our bond. I was blindly in love and ready to do anything to make your father happy. There was just one doubt nagging my mind—I hadn't told Vishwamitra my real identity!'

'You lied to him for a decade?' Shakuntala asked incredulously.

Menaka nodded unhappily. 'I'm not proud of it but I knew the truth would anger him and ruin the precious bond we had. It was the only genuine relationship I have ever had with a man. I would have lied all my life if it meant we could enjoy that bliss together!'

'Why didn't you?' Shakuntala demanded. 'Why couldn't you have continued the lie for another ten years and let me enjoy the warmth of your affection as well?'

Menaka wiped a tear that had escaped her eye and said, 'I wish things were that simple, my child. When you truly love someone it becomes imperative that you share your deepest secrets with them. I couldn't bear to live with the guilt of

having deceived him any more. I thought . . . I was mistaken.'
She paused, then continued with a sigh, 'I thought he would
forgive my transgression but he lashed out at me with all his
anger. I left completely heartbroken and gave birth to you
alone in the forest.'

Shakuntala had tears in her own eyes now. 'So you
decided to abandon me? Hoping that the wild beasts of the
forest would make a meal out of me and rid you of the sign of
your failed affair once and for all?'

'No, Shakuntala,' Menaka pleaded, 'I left you for your own
good! Had I taken you to Swarg, you would have led the same
lifestyle as I did. I could never wish that for you. I couldn't
abandon you in the forest so I left you outside the hermitage
of Maharishi Kanav. I watched till someone noticed your
presence and took you inside. Every single cell of my body
longed to hold you in my arms. Turning away from you was
the hardest thing I have ever done.'

When Shakuntala didn't respond, Menaka continued in a
soft voice, 'Despite my efforts to save you from the heartbreak
that I experienced, the fate gods have conspired against you.
Trust me, my child, you need my help now more than ever . . .
the seed of the Chandravanshis has taken root inside you and
I couldn't let you deal with this difficult situation by yourself!'

Shakuntala looked at her mother in horror and Menaka
nodded weakly, 'Yes, my child, you are carrying the next heir
of Hastinapur in your womb.'

Dushyant

Adhyaye 11

Dushyant had never imagined that kingship would bring so many responsibilities with it. In the absence of his father's guidance, the entire burden of running the kingdom was on his young shoulders especially since his brothers, who had joined the council, were as inexperienced as him.

To make matters worse, as Parshu-Raam's campaign against corrupt Kshatriyas moved out of Nabhi-varsh, barbarians from other countries flocked to it, seeking refuge there! Ironically, since the Avatar was already done with it, Nabhi-varsh was turning out to be the safest place for them to hide.

'What good is Lord Parshu-Raam's mission if it leads to the barbarians invading us? Wasn't he supposed to drive them off the planet once and for all?' Dushyant vented his frustration before the kulguru and the royal court.

The kulguru understood the reasons for Dushyant's outburst and said calmly, 'Such doubts do not suit a young warrior of Dharma. Bhargav Raam's campaign of cleansing the earth is still in its early stages. We tend to think of only our kingdoms and our country but he has vowed to rid the *entire* earth of evil and tyrant kings. His vision is of a global nature and it is our duty to support him in this endeavour.'

Dushyant knew Dirghatamas was right but he still resented the unwanted burden. 'Gurudev,' he protested, 'it has put so much pressure on our kingdom! There are skirmishes all along our northern and western borders. How am I supposed to face this onslaught with half the positions in our army still vacant?'

'I agree. Their assault does put us in a precarious position but what do you have to fear? You have four strong, capable brothers who can protect the four borders of our kingdom, why not distribute the responsibility amongst them?'

Dushyant looked at his brothers who were a part of the meeting. Each of them signalled their readiness but he shook his head and said, 'I don't want to send them into a fight while I sit here in the safety of the palace. Vasu shall take care of the kingdom while I personally go to the northern mountains that are facing the worst onslaught.'

The kulguru nodded in approval—his protégé was beginning to take ownership of the kingdom. However, he countered the king's words and said, 'I appreciate your sense of fairness, my king, but I would advise you to stay in the capital for the time being. You have been crowned recently and the citizens need to get used to seeing you as the head of this kingdom. Send your brothers to deal with the nuisance while you maintain control from the capital. There shall be enough opportunities in the future for you to fight.'

Dushyant realized the wisdom of the acharya's words and accepted the suggestion.

Dirghatamas began elaborating the plan, 'I suggest Bhim take one-fourth of the army to the north while another one-fourth goes with Shoor to the western border. Divide another one-fourth amongst Pravasu and Vasu and send them to relieve their brothers after a fortnight. The rest of the force should be positioned around Hastinapur under your control to take care of any unexpected rebellions in the city.'

The king agreed it was a good plan and his concern about securing his borders lessened a little. True, he was inexperienced himself, but he did have people like Acharya Dirghatamas to guide him. The discussion was interrupted by the announcement of a guest, a female guest, who had arrived from the forests and wished to see the king. Dushyant was momentarily confused but then his heart began to beat faster. Could it be Shakuntala?

While Dushyant had been embroiled in the machinations of statecraft, Shakuntala had decided to take matters into her own hands. Menaka had shocked her with the revelation that she was carrying a child and had informed her that due to her celestial ancestry, the baby may have accelerated growth. Shakuntala was dreading the prospect of breaking the news to her father but fortunately, Maharishi Kanav once again proved supportive and sent her to Hastinapur with two of his most trusted acolytes. Her baby bump had already begun to show and her heart beat with apprehension as she entered the city.

Dushyant's ring helped her gain entry into the palace, where she was escorted to the royal sabha of the Purus. She walked slowly towards the moon throne, looking at the new king of Hastinapur with mixed emotions. Dushyant looked splendid in his royal robes and tall silver crown. His handsome face sported a fine moustache that enhanced his regal bearing. In spite of the resentment she harboured towards him, Shakuntala reluctantly acknowledged that he was looking wonderful.

Dushyant recognized her immediately. As he gazed upon her once again, he wondered how he could have forgotten her ethereal beauty. Clad in a simple mauve sari and completely devoid of ornaments, Shakuntala could still put the royal women of Hastinapur to shame. What was she doing here?

Shakuntala saw the expressions on his face change—the initial flicker of recognition was replaced quickly by confusion—and all her misgivings returned as she saw him trying to avoid her gaze.

Addressing him directly, she said in a bold voice, 'Greetings to the king of Hastinapur and the royal council from the daughter of Maharishi Kanav.'

She had given her introduction for the benefit of the council and saw that they were impressed. Maharishi Kanav was renowned as one of the seers whose compositions were a part of the Vedic corpus. All the councillors folded their hands in greeting. Except Dushyant.

When the king did not react to her salutation, Acharya Dirghatamas responded politely, 'Hastinapur welcomes the daughter of the venerable Maharishi. Pray tell us, child, how is your father and for what purpose has he sent you here?'

Shakuntala turned to answer the guru, 'My father is well, Acharya, and he has sent me here to remind the king of a promise he had made while visiting our ashram.'

The ministers looked at their king inquiringly; they were too polite to ask anything directly so they waited for the situation to reveal itself. The kulguru realized something was amiss when the king still did not respond.

Dushyant knew he had wronged Shakuntala by cutting off all communication, but the guilt of not being there for his father had not left his heart completely. In the time that Shakuntala and Dirghatamas had been exchanging pleasantries, he had made up his mind about how he would react to her unannounced arrival—he would deny being aware of her very existence.

'I do not understand what the lady here is implying,' he finally said. 'Have you been sent here to ask for money? If so, please let us know how much you need and I shall order the treasurer to sanction the required amount. If you are here to ask for cattle I shall be glad to send a hundred of our best cows for the Maharishi's ashram.'

Shakuntala controlled her rising anger and responded boldly, 'Perhaps the king doesn't realize that hermits do not subsist on money. We have enough cattle of our own and we eat and breathe Dharma for a living. Our lives are spent in fulfilling our duties to the gods and the countless life forms around us. A concept that clearly seems to be alien to our king, for he even refuses to acknowledge the girl he himself chose as his wife!'

The entire council gasped at the statement and the kulguru shook his head in dismay. Dushyant had hoped that Shakuntala would leave after seeing his indifference, but now that she had revealed the most damning thing she could have, he had to refute her claim and destroy her credibility.

'What kind of insidious allegation is this?' he thundered. 'I have never even seen you in the kingdom before, let alone take you for wife.'

Mortified, Shakuntala wondered how she could have chosen such a man for her husband. She knew he was cleverly twisting his words to reveal half-truths. She replied with trembling lips, 'Yes, you have never seen me in *your* kingdom, but you did seek refuge in *my* hermitage after losing your way in the forest! Knowing everything, how can you, a scion of Puruvansh, the king of Hastinapur, talk like a base person?'

Dushyant's face turned red with embarrassment. He blurted out, 'I didn't even know of your existence till now! How could I have married you? What kind of charlatan are you?'

Shakuntala was livid now. 'You think that you alone have knowledge of your deeds? He who sins, thinking that no one has observed him, forgets that he is always watched by Shri Hari Vishnu residing within his heart. The sun and the moon, the five elements, day, night, and Yamraj himself witness the acts of men. By rejecting me today, you have definitely earned their ire, O great Chandravanshi king!'

Dirghatamas was confused—the girl seemed to be genuinely disturbed, but at the same time the king was vociferously denying any involvement with her. He remembered the conversation he had had with Dushyant in the crematorium and knew it was possible that Shakuntala was telling the truth. But why wasn't Dushyant acknowledging it?

He decided to intervene and said softly, 'Maharaj, it does not behove the king of Hastinapur to talk to any woman in this manner. The lady is the foster daughter of Maharishi Kanav and her birth parents are Brahmarishi Vishwamitra and the celestial Apsara Menaka. I find it difficult to be a part of such a denigration of womanhood.'

Dushyant hated himself for what he was about to do but he had to finish what he had started. He stood up from the throne in a huff and said, 'Ah! So you are the infamous spawn of that celestial whore Menaka's dalliance with the lustful Vishwamitra? No wonder you've come here today to fulfil some twisted fantasy of yours. This is the Puru court, woman, not a dancing house where your histrionics will be appreciated. Go and find someone foolish enough to believe your lies!'

A wave of desolation hit her almost like a physical blow and Shakuntala swayed where she stood. Dushyant was using the past, over which she had no control, to ruin her present and future, to demean her in front of his guru and councillors. He was beyond redemption.

Vowing to destroy his arrogance, she said in a calm voice that belied the storm inside her, 'You perceive others' shortcomings so well, O great king, yet you are completely blind to your own faults. What can be more preposterous than the wicked defaming the honest? Truth is the biggest virtue, Truth is God Himself! Since you have chosen to lie and disavow your lawfully wedded wife, I must depart from here immediately. My mother Menaka is a celestial and my father is the first king in the history of mankind to have attained the title of Brahmarishi—my birth, thus, is higher than yours. I spit on the crown that gives you this sense of self-importance.' She curled her hand protectively over her belly. 'You will not get away with insulting me thus, Maharaj Dushyant. Even now the heir to the moon throne is quickening in my womb, and I swear to raise him as your arch-enemy from the moment he is born. Should the need arise I shall not hesitate to seek the help of my nephew Parshu-Raam, the scourge of all wicked kings. I shall finish what you have started here today, Dushyant!'

Adhyaye 12

As she walked out of the Puru palace with bold steps, Shakuntala began to shed the bitter tears of one whose heart has been broken for the very first time.

How could Dushyant not recognize his soulmate? Didn't he know they were meant to spend their lives together? She had hoped that seeing her walk out of the hall—and his life—would bring him to his senses. That he would run after her to stop her, embrace her and say he was sorry. But as she stepped out, there was only a stunned silence behind her.

Having been forsaken by the very man who was supposed to have welcomed her with open arms, she realized she had nowhere to go. The two hermits who had accompanied her from the forest had already left after bringing her to the palace. Had it been a matter of just herself, she would have returned to her father's ashram, but now she had to worry about the child who was being denied his destiny as well. She would not rest till Dushyant fell at her feet to apologize and establish her offspring on the moon throne. She sighed deeply as she walked out of the city gates—it was going to be a long winter.

Fortunately, the woods outside Hastinapur were home to many mendicants and she soon found refuge after she introduced herself as the daughter of Maharishi Kanav. As the skies darkened, she huddled beside a small fire, trying to shield herself from the cool winds that had begun blowing. An old lady offered her a blanket and Shakuntala gratefully accepted.

The physical exhaustion of the journey and the emotional trauma she had experienced in the palace took their toll and she slipped into a fitful slumber. Perhaps she had been too eager to see a fulfilment of her own desires in Dushyant's arrival; her house had been burnt by a fire of her own making. Her imagination fuelled by the thoughts of regret and retribution, she began having a fantastic dream.

The darkness of Prithvi had been replaced by the glow of two suns revolving languidly around each other and she felt herself being borne along on gossamer clouds. They rose higher and higher, taking her to a golden planet enveloped in crimson and pink-hued mist, and towards a set of massive doors guarded by multi-limbed creatures. She felt a little afraid but they barely glanced at her and the majestic gates slowly opened to allow her inside.

She was gliding through wide streets lined by impressive palaces. The inhabitants of those grand citadels watched as she passed by. It was hard to make out their expressions, but they seemed to be looking at her in wonder and excitement. Slowly, she felt the anger and disappointment of the court melt away, to be replaced by a warm feeling of belonging. She was surrounded by people who cared for her and her eyes filled with tears of gratitude.

She felt the gentle touch of someone's hand on her arm and was startled to see her mother floating by her side. Menaka smiled at her, nodding in assurance, and Shakuntala felt as if all her worries had been pulled away. The fragrant wind gently guided her to a nearby mountain that was glittering with jewels of all imaginable colours. Multiple rainbows shimmered in the air in the light from the two suns and sparkling cascades splashed from the mountain to form massive pools at its base.

For a moment, she was reminded of her own home in the foothills of the Himalayas. But this was like no landscape on earth. The trees, with their silver bark and enormous golden leaves, were taller than any she had ever seen. The branches were laden with flowers in shades of crimson, orange, scarlet, pink, peach, mauve, lavender, yellow . . . and many others she could not name. Butterflies of all possible shapes and sizes flitted about, spreading the multi-coloured pollen in the wind.

At the pinnacle of the mountain the trees cleared to give her a glimpse of an iridescent palace. In complete contrast to the colourful surroundings, the palace was stark white, with spires so tall that it seemed they would pierce the edge of the heavens. She had barely begun to admire its intricate architecture when she was whizzed into a hexagonal hall that was larger than the entire palace of Hastinapur.

The floor was made of some transparent material that she could not recognize. At the other end of the hall was what looked like a huge dragon. At first she was alarmed at the sight of the creature, but as she got closer, she realized it was just a life-size replica that served as a throne. And on it sat the most handsome man she had ever seen in her life. He had a high forehead bearing the mark of a thunderbolt, large olive-green eyes, dark wavy hair and a perfect nose sitting above bow-shaped lips. Pristine white robes accentuated his well-built body and a crown of diamonds adorned his head.

Shakuntala knew she had seen or read about him somewhere but her thoughts were too fluid to form any shape. A huge elephant, white as the snow, stood next to the throne, shaking his three heads in mirth. Three heads! Shakuntala's mind registered the anomaly momentarily, but then it was lost in the warm fuzzy feeling that was filling her brain. On the other side of the dragon throne was a unicorn of the same flawless milky white colour. When it saw her, it stamped its hooves in excitement, tossing its golden mane.

Her subconscious mind finally processed all the information pouring in—the presence of her mother next to her, the shimmering landscape, the beautiful and happy people, the handsome man on the dragon throne, the six-tusked elephant, the flying unicorn . . . She was in Swarg, the heavenly abode of Indra. Indra, the leader of the Devas, who slew the dragon Vritra with his Vajra, and rode Airavat, the white elephant, and Ucchaishrava, the unicorn!

The surprise she felt at the revelation was replaced by wonder as a stunning rainbow appeared behind the three. Suddenly she became aware of the sound of flapping wings and found herself surrounded by countless Vidyadhars dressed in the same pristine white. One by one, they began offering her lavender lotuses and soon her hands were full of the blooms. Still they kept giving her more, greeting her in lilting voices that were like the tinkling of temple bells. They guided her to a sparkling lake just outside the hall where they bathed and clothed her in garments studded with precious gems.

When she emerged from the pool the natural glow of her skin had been restored and all signs of the previous weeks of anxiety had been wiped from her visage. The Apsaras arrived with her mother and began to adorn her with ornaments, showering her with soft, delicate petals and singing songs of fertility and blessings. She smiled when she realized what was happening—in the absence of her family, the celestials were performing the Garbha Sanskar ceremony to bless the unborn child. Their concern and thoughtfulness overwhelmed her.

Abruptly, she noticed a small ficus leaf, the colour of a monsoon cloud, come floating towards her from amongst the petals around her. She was surprised, and though she jerked in her sleep she couldn't open her eyes until the ceremony was completed. The leaf was slowly being absorbed into her skin, passing through her abdomen and she could sense it form a protective layer around her womb.

And then, in the dream, she saw her baby and a wave of relief passed through her entire being. He was bursting with health—thickly lashed eyes, a slightly upturned nose, ringlets of dark hair on his head and lightly curled fingers and toes. The mark of Shri Hari Vishnu's chakra was appearing on the palm of his right hand while a lotus whorl was taking shape on the sole of his left foot. She realized that it would not take her ten lunar months to birth the child; her half-Apsara body had hastened the growth of the babe in her womb. A name reverberated in her mind: Sarvadaman, the subduer of all.

In that blissful state of semi-consciousness, tears rolled down her eyes as she felt all the laments of the past and the anxiety for the future disappear. She was not alone after all . . .

The gods were looking after mother and child.

Adhyaye 13

Harishchandra had adjusted to life in the crematorium quite well. While the next Chandravanshi life was taking root in Hastinapur, the Suryavanshi king was learning new things about death in Kanyakubja.

To his relief, he had been asked to manage only the monetary affairs of the ceremony, not anything morbid. What surprised him was the fact that even the departed were required to pay taxes. On his first day when he had asked Veerbahu, the chandal had smiled and taken Harishchandra into the cremation ground. It was a large square plot of land with a boundary wall running along the perimeter and a couple of rooms in one corner. There was a well to draw underground water and a shrine dedicated to Lord Shiva in the northeast corner. The two sat down on the steps of the small temple, and the chandal explained, 'Even after the soul departs, the body still needs to be disposed of properly. We can't let it rot like an animal's corpse. It must be taken care of in a way that doesn't release any diseases into the environment. Arrangements have to be made to procure the wood for the pyre, clarified butter, flowers, cloth, and other paraphernalia. All this requires money.' Harishchandra had nodded sombrely; he had never thought about such matters before. Veerbahu would frequently travel out of the city and in time Harishchandra got used to managing the affairs of the establishment by himself.

He was finishing the fourth week of work today, and as darkness began spreading its invisible cloak over the landscape, he reflected on the past month. It occurred to him then that he had learnt a lot more in the days he had spent away from the throne than he had in his years on it. He had missed his family and was looking forward to going back to Ayodhya with the duration of his servitude ending tonight. His body had become gaunt and his face was half covered with an unkempt beard, yet taking care of his impermanent frame had not seemed to matter where he was. The calculation of levies had been easy enough, but the cries of mourners still unsettled him. As he watched the embers on the last pyre die, he was relieved that he wouldn't have to hear the heart-rending screams of the living again.

And it wasn't just the living who screamed in the dead of the night. At times, when he woke up at some odd hour, he could hear whispering and crying that couldn't have come from any human. Veerbahu had told him about spirits that clung to the material world especially of people who had died sudden, unnatural deaths. Unwilling to let go of their material desires, those unfortunate souls were trapped in the mortal realm. The chandal had even told him that the cries Harishchandra heard in the night were the screams of the spirits he was trying to get under his control.

Harishchandra wasn't a superstitious man, but after spending a month in the crematorium, he could believe almost anything. It was a cool night, and he wrapped the coarse blanket he had been given around him. Every evening, before retiring to his small room, he made sure that all the fires had been extinguished. Just as he was about to do the same today, he observed the dim outline of a figure standing at the gates. Veerbahu had already retired for the night so he took a torch from its bracket and hurried towards the entrance. For some reason an unnamed dread was filling his heart.

It was a woman, holding a lifeless body in her arms. As he neared her, the light from the torch fell on her face, and he gasped—it was his wife, Tara! His heart picked up pace and he rushed to see who she was holding, hoping that it wasn't who he feared it was.

'No, no, no! This cannot be!' he shouted in agony.

In a moment that seemed frozen in time, he stood rooted at the spot, unable to tear his eyes from the spectre of his wife clutching the lifeless body of their only child. He had watched countless people in the past month mourn their dead and had tried to harden his heart to their anguish, but now, his heart shattered at the sight of his own son's dead body. He stumbled under the weight of his grief as he took Rohitashwa into his arms, frantically trying to revive him in a futile effort. Tears streaming down his face, he looked at his wife. 'Tara! What happened to our son?'

Taramati was in no condition to say anything. The torch that had fallen on the ground gave her a surreal glow and she looked as if she was in a daze. Harishchandra gently placed his son's lifeless form down and shook her shoulders. As her eyes roved over his face, the erstwhile queen took a moment to recognize him, and then burst out sobbing. 'I am so sorry I could not take care of our son.'

Harishchandra took her in his arms to calm her. 'Shhh! I am sure it wasn't your fault, Tara. Tell me what happened.'

His wife narrated the events of the day to him, 'Today was the end of our month in Kanyakubja, and I was so excited about seeing you tomorrow. While I was packing our belongings, Rohit went out to the orchard to get some fruits for our journey back home. When I was done, I went and paid the innkeeper all his remaining dues and asked him to arrange for our travel. It was then that I realized Rohit hadn't come back, so I went looking for him. It was already late afternoon. When I finally found him, he was lying under the mango tree. I thought he must have dozed off after climbing the trees and eating the fruit.'

Harishchandra's heart was breaking with every word his wife uttered. Just a few hours ago he had been contemplating the return to Ayodhya with his family but it seemed destiny had some more pain and misery in store for them. Taramati had been so strong all this while, taking care of their child in an unknown city while he was completely cut off from her.

Fresh tears sprang from her eyes as she told him what happened next. 'I touched him lightly to wake him and when he didn't get up I turned him around. He was frothing from the mouth!' she cried. 'He'd been bitten by a snake! I tried my best to revive him but couldn't do anything. The innkeeper helped me take him to the vaidya, but he said it was too late. I had to bring him here . . .' Her words ended in a broken whisper.

'Why are you carrying Rohit alone? Why didn't the innkeeper come with you?' Harishchandra asked.

Taramati replied in a choked voice, 'The inn was overflowing with visitors and I couldn't wait for him. I had to bring Rohit here before nightfall so I carried him here myself.'

Harishchandra nodded. 'Rohit's body has turned blue. We need to cremate him immediately.' It was heart-wrenching for him to say the words, but they had to do what was required. He quickly made a list of everything that would be needed and, calculating the cost, told Tara with a heavy heart, 'I am obliged to ask for the dues necessary to cremate our child. Do you have anything that I can offer as payment to my employer?'

Taramati was stunned. *How could he ask for money to cremate his own child!* She looked into his distressed eyes that were torn between his duty towards the only man who had hired him in this strange city, and his own family. She answered in a hopeless voice, 'I don't have anything. The little we had was used to pay for our lodging and food in the past month, and to secure our travel for tomorrow.'

Harishchandra shook his head in despair, 'My employer has asked me to collect the dues in advance. I cannot make an exception because it is someone from my family. I know I am being heartless, Tara, but this man helped me when no one else would!'

'He is *your* son, Maharaj!' Tara cried balefully and slumped to the ground. Harishchandra remained standing, unable to do anything to help her. His heart was heavy with the loss of his only child; the son for whom he had invited the wrath of Vishwamitra, upset Brahmarishi Vasishth, and almost committed the heinous crime of Nar-bali.

A sudden desire to rid himself of the trappings of the material world arose in his mind and he told his wife, 'Since I am the one responsible for our miseries leading up to this cursed night, I shall find a way out of our predicament. I shall offer my life as payment for our son's cremation and shall remain in this place till my last breath.'

Tara was aghast at his statement and tried to dissuade him. She had already lost her son; she could not lose her husband as well. But Harishchandra's mind was made up and he wouldn't listen. With determined steps, he walked to Veerbahu's room, but before he could knock, the door opened on its own. Harishchandra glanced up and was stunned to see Brahmarishi Vishwamitra instead of the chandal!

The Suryavanshi staggered backward in confusion. 'How? What? How are you here, Brahmarishi?'

Vishwamitra said to him reassuringly, 'Do not be alarmed, Harishchandra. All this was just an assessment of your true character. Every small or big ordeal that you have been through, beginning with my usurpation of the Suryavanshi throne, leading up to tonight, has been a test to see how much you have evolved from the time I first met you.'

Both Harishchandra and Tara were flabbergasted by Vishwamitra's revelation and looked at him in bewilderment.

'I had promised Parshu-Raam that you were a reformed man, but I wanted to judge for myself if that was indeed true. I also owed it to my mentor, Brahmarishi Vasishth, to ensure that you would not put him in a similar situation if faced with a crisis again.'

Harishchandra fell down at the guru's feet, weeping bitterly. 'What kind of test is this, Gurudev? Our indebtedness to you was for saving the life of the same boy who now lies dead in front of our eyes. Your examination took away the only thing I value in this world, my lord! What use is the throne of Ayodhya to me now?'

Vishwamitra gave him an enigmatic smile and gestured towards where the prince's body lay. When the couple turned, they saw their son rising from the ground as if he was getting up from sleep!

The Brahmarishi patted Harishchandra's head and said, 'Rohit was never dead, my king. The snake venom had only put him in a state of paralysis. Everything that has happened in Kanyakubja was a step towards making all of you better people. You and your family have shed your pride and ego. You worked hard to repay me with the money you earned yourself while your wife helped in the inn and cared for Rohit in a truly commendable fashion. Even young Rohit here has turned from a pampered prince into a well-behaved though occasionally naughty boy!'

He beamed with pride at the people who were still giving him baffled looks. 'Seeing the devotion towards duty you have shown tonight,' Vishwamitra declared, 'I hereby free you from all your debts. It is time for you to go back to Kosal and take over the reins of the kingdom. I relinquish my place on the Suryavanshi throne and humbly resign from my post of chief preceptor.'

Harishchandra embraced his family through tears of joy and relief. Their ordeal was finally over. Then, with folded hands, he turned towards Vishwamitra and said, 'You stepped into our lives to save us from the unpardonable sins of Brahma-hatya and Nar-bali. You protected us from the wrath of Bhagwan Parshu-Raam and have taught us a most valuable lesson as only a true teacher could have. I accept the throne, Gurudev, but you cannot deprive Ayodhya of your guidance!'

Vishwamitra smiled at the king. 'My part in your destiny is over, Rajan. Just as you have atoned for your sins here, Brahmarishi Vasishth's penance is also complete. He is on his way to Ayodhya even as we speak and shall be there to welcome you back to your city. Go, and live the rest of your life in accordance with the principles of Dharma.'

He blessed the royal family of Ayodhya and marched out of the crematorium. By testing Harishchandra's adherence to Dharma, Vishwamitra had fulfilled his obligation to Brahmarishi Vasishth who was a mentor to both of them. Now, it was time for him to settle the debt he owed his daughter.

Adhyaye 14

Menaka had watched over her daughter with a deep sadness. The nine months of gestation had been condensed into just nine weeks and with no one else to take care of the mother-to-be, she had decided to step in.

Sweet birdsong competed with the cries of the newborn as she now sat beside Shakuntala, cradling the child. Her eyes filled with tears as she held her grandson in her arms. Sarvadaman was the perfect blend of Dushyant and Shakuntala and his grandmother was in love with him already.

Shakuntala noticed the tears in her mother's eyes and expressed her gratitude, 'Although you abandoned me when I was a baby, you saved my son today. I am sorry I was rude to you when you came to me offering help. You are the only one who cared for me in this condition and warned me of what to expect!'

'Hush! Don't stress yourself, child,' Menaka said, patting her daughter's hand. 'I had warned you about the baby's development precisely to make you aware of the possibility of such a situation arising. I was watching over you throughout your journey and the subsequent events in the court of Hastinapur. Even I hadn't expected the baby to be born so soon but perhaps the shock of the incident was enough to precipitate his birth. I dare say he may actually grow faster than other children as well!'

Shakuntala had resigned herself to circumstances. She turned to Menaka and said, 'Mother, I would like to go back to the hermitage as soon as possible. I want to go far away from this wretched city to a place where I can provide a safe and secure environment for my son. The day I see him sitting on the moon throne shall be the happiest day of my life and I must do everything in my power to train him for that.'

Menaka's forehead creased into a frown at the last statement and she asked gently, 'Shakuntala, must you consume yourself with the thought of vengeance so?'

Her daughter replied with a question of her own. 'Was it easy for you to forgive Brahmarishi Vishwamitra after he threw you out of his ashram?'

Menaka didn't respond immediately but she understood what her daughter was implying. Shakuntala's hurt would not be forgotten so easily. Perhaps with time she would forget the devastating impact of Dushyant's behaviour but right now it was too soon. She nodded and kissed the head of the small, flushed baby who was drifting in and out of sleep while Shakuntala pushed her point.

'I will keep the fire of retribution burning within my heart. I have promised Dushyant that I shall avenge my insult through my child and I shall spend my life training him for the fight.'

Menaka was alarmed at her daughter's determination. Not forgiving Dushyant was one thing but Shakuntala's obsession with revenge would put too great a burden on the child. Deciding to take an indirect approach to the subject, she said in a casual tone, 'You know, there is an interesting story about my friend Matali that I am reminded of right now. Do you want to hear it?'

'Of course,' Shakuntala said, eager to talk about something else; anything was better than thinking about the man who had shown her lofty dreams and then snubbed her so cruelly in front of his entire council.

'I am not sure if you are aware, but Matali is the chief pilot of Indra's vimans. He has a beautiful daughter called Gunakeshi. This story is about the time when he was searching for a suitable bridegroom for her. Gunakeshi was rather proud of her looks, and did not wish to settle for anyone in Swarg, unlike her friends. She had heard fascinating tales about the wealth and splendour of the lower lokas and urged her father to find someone better looking than her friends' suitors. Being the doting father that he was, Matali was left with no choice but to do as she asked.'

Shakuntala interrupted with a question, 'Are the inhabitants of the lower lokas really more opulent and beautiful? I had assumed the netherworlds were filled with horrible Asurs and monsters!'

'Well, my child,' Menaka said with a smile, 'beauty lies in the eyes of the beholder. In Swarg, where everyone is good-looking, one's outer magnificence ceases to be relevant and it is one's personality that defines their beauty. The denizens of the lower lokas look no different from us, though their descriptions make them sound horrible. But they don't have to be hideous just because they are Asurs, and sharing from personal experience, some of them are quite attractive in fact!'

Shakuntala smiled at the confession and wondered how many Asurs her mother had met in her life. Menaka ignored her daughter's inquisitive smile and continued with the story.

'Matali took the help of Devarishi Narad who is the only being who can travel through all fourteen lokas with impunity. They began their tour with Varun's domain at the bottom of the ocean, where Narad pointed out Pushkar, the prince of the Matsya or mer-people.'

'Oh! The mer-people are real then?' Shakuntala asked in surprise, 'I always thought they were just fables told to send children to sleep.'

Her mother nodded and replied, 'Of course they are real! Surely you didn't think that your planet, three quarters of which is water, would not have any intelligent life in it! See, that is the problem with you humans—you are so full of scepticism that you fail to see the magic that is all around you!'

'I understand, Mother,' Shakuntala said, raising her hands defensively, 'can we get on with the story now?'

Menaka sighed. 'Matali was impressed by the boy's good looks, except for the slight issue of him having a fish's tail instead of legs! Narad assured Matali that this problem was easily dealt with—mer-people could develop feet when they were on land, and revert to their original form when in the water. However, it so happened that Pushkar was already betrothed to Jyotsna, the daughter of the moon god, and so he said no to their proposal gracefully.'

Shakuntala was mesmerized by the descriptions of the other-world creatures. 'How I wish I could travel to these places sometimes!' she burst out.

'Who knows! You may well do it some day because of your child!' Menaka said, smiling at her enthusiasm. 'To move on with the story, the two then decided to head to Hiranyapur, the capital city of Patal, where Narad pointed out many suitable Daityas and Danavs. However, Matali wasn't convinced. The Devas and Asurs, although half-brothers, had always been hostile to each other. What would Indra say if his own charioteer wed his daughter to a Danav prince? He was also well aware of Narad's penchant for causing trouble, so he refused and urged him to move to the next loka.

'In Naga-loka Matali spotted a well-built and handsome Naga. When he inquired about him, Narad shook his head and said that although the chosen Naga, Sumukh, belonged to a noble family, he was doomed to die soon. Unknown to him, the Naga had been marked by Garud as his prey.'

'Looks like your friend Matali did choose the right companion for the trip after all,' Shakuntala said in wonder. 'How can these sages know so much about everybody and have so much power? I have even heard of rishis like Durvasa and Bhrigu cursing the Devas!'

'Well, my child,' Menaka answered patiently, 'it is because most of these rishis are even older than the Devas themselves. The Sanat Kumars, Atri, Angiras, Bhrigu, Vasishth and Narad, among others, came into being before Brahma created the Devas and Asurs and therefore hold more authority than either clan.

'Moving on with our story,' she said, 'Matali was completely frustrated with his fruitless search for a groom. Feeling sorry for the Naga who would soon become a meal for the divine eagle in the prime of his youth, he decided to ignore Narad's advice to let nature take its course, and informed the young boy of the fate that awaited him. However, he did have a proposition—if Sumukh agreed to marry his daughter, Matali himself would request Indra to save his life.'

Shakuntala could imagine the scenario and said smiling, 'I am sure he would have said yes even if Gunakeshi was an ugly old hag!'

Menaka laughed. 'Perhaps! Luckily for him she was a very pretty albeit pampered girl. As you rightly guessed, Sumukh agreed to the proposal and Matali rushed back to Swarg to convince Indra to intercede in the matter. Unable to refuse his loyal charioteer, Indra decided to give a portion of Amrit, the elixir of immortality, to the Naga.'

'Indra did that for his *charioteer*?' Shakuntala was incredulous.

'Yes, you do not know what a large heart he has! I don't talk to him too often since the episode with your father, but Shakra is one of the best Indras that have sat on the throne of heaven.'

The knowledge gave Shakuntala heart, for wasn't it the same Deva who had blessed her in the dream?

Looking at her daughter's thoughtful expression, Menaka asked, 'You do know that Indra keeps changing?'

'Of course, Mother,' Shakuntala huffed, 'we are still in the Tretayug. The wisdom of the scriptures isn't lost to us yet! I know that "Indra" is a title for the leader of the gods and just like the kings on earth, Indra also keeps changing. Currently, that post is held by Shakra, the eldest son of Rishi Kashyap and Mother Aditi, hence he is also known as the leader of the Adityas.'

Menaka nodded in appreciation and continued, 'So, due to Matali's intervention, Sumukh was now an immortal. When the mighty Garud heard what had happened, he was inflamed with anger, and marched on Indra's capital Amravati.'

Shakuntala interrupted her by saying, 'If I am not mistaken, isn't Garud Shakra's stepbrother? Wasn't the story of his birth also related to Indra upsetting some rishis?'

Her mother sighed and said, 'That's true. Shakra used to be quite impetuous in his younger days, and I dare say, that trait hasn't left him completely still. But that's a story for another time. Garud met Indra and rebuked him, saying, "You were the one who gave me the boon to feed on Nagas and now you yourself are stealing my meal, brother! I can bear the weight of the three worlds on a single wing, something even you cannot do. Just because I bear Lord Vishnu on my back doesn't make me a servant who can be treated shabbily!"'

Shakuntala was surprised at that; there was a definite hint of arrogance in Garud's tone and Menaka confirmed the same.

'Hearing his proud words Indra told his stepbrother that the three worlds together could not bear the weight of Lord Hari if he didn't wish it. That it was only through the Lord's mercy that Garud could bear him so he should not give in to false pride. Of course, that did not go down well with the mighty eagle. There followed a fierce scuffle between the two in which they were soon joined by their respective clans. Many Devas and Garuds sustained grievous injuries in the ensuing battle. It was only when Shri Hari Vishnu Himself intervened, that peace was restored to Swarg.'

'But what happened to Sumukh and Gunakeshi?'

'They did get married but only after the battle was over and many others had lost their lives in the process. Gunakeshi's yearnings made her pester her father to travel to different lokas in search of a suitable groom. For her sake, Matali was forced to interfere with the natural flow of events to change the life of one person. This led to a battle of egos between the king of the gods and the king of the birds which resulted in great destruction on both the sides.'

She fixed her daughter with a steady gaze and said, 'The desire for something that is not meant for us can ruin not just our own lives, but can also have far-reaching consequences for others. Even the flapping of a butterfly's wings can cause a storm somewhere else.'

Shakuntala understood Menaka's unsaid words—her mother hoped she wouldn't destroy the life of her own son in the quest for revenge.

Adhyaye 15

Dushyant had realized his mistake the moment Shakuntala had stepped out of his palace but he didn't know what to do about it after having humiliated her so terribly. For the past few weeks his conscience had been gnawing at him and he had been completely disinterested in everything around him. He would walk out of meetings abruptly, ignoring all protocol, and would be found sitting aloof in some part of the garden. Eventually he even stopped attending court.

Finally, Acharya Dirghatamas decided to step in.

When the king pleaded ill-health for the third day in a row, the kulguru came to meet him. Seeing Dushyant's miserable condition, he said softly, 'My king, things cannot go on like this. Your absence in court has been noticed. Everyone in the council is worried.'

When Dushyant didn't respond Dirghatamas touched his arm gently and said, 'The incident with Maharishi Kanav's daughter has clearly affected you more than you let on, my son. Since the day Shakuntala stormed out of the court, you have stopped caring for things you used to love. The royal cooks have reported that you have not been eating well and the stable boys also mentioned that you

89

haven't taken your favourite steeds out for a ride in several weeks.'

When the king still did not respond, he decided to change tack. 'Shakuntala is no ordinary hermit girl, Rajan. If it was just dalliance you had in mind it would have been more prudent to choose one of the courtesans rather than an innocent girl unschooled in the ways of the world. I didn't intervene at that time because I couldn't ascertain the veracity of her claims but your current state has removed all my doubts. I'm disappointed in your conduct—'

The words seemed to strike a chord inside Dushyant's mind and he responded with feeling, 'Please do not say that, Gurudev! You have raised me to follow the path of Dharma since I was a child, how could you think that I would stoop so low? It was not my intention to *use* her . . . I love Shakuntala! It was the guilt of not being here for my father that drove me to ignore her after I returned from the ashram. Her sudden arrival caught me by surprise; I didn't know how to react. That made me behave in a completely foolish and unforgivable manner but I know it is not an excuse. What I did was abominable and I am ashamed of it.'

Dushyant knew he had run away from his personal responsibilities by refusing to recognize Shakuntala. He had to face his demons else he would never be able to sleep in peace. 'I was too proud to admit my mistake all this while,' he told Dirghatamas, 'but I cannot take it any more. Please tell me how to undo the pain I have caused her and make things right again.'

Dirghatamas was glad that his protégé had finally opened up. Patting Dushyant's hand, he said, 'If a person truly wants to absolve himself of a past sin, he has to atone for it through his actions in the present. The only way to make amends for your behaviour is to approach the lady and beg for her understanding. Invite her back to the royal court with full honours and declare her as your lawfully wedded wife in front of the whole council and the citizens.'

Dushyant nodded and said, 'But I don't even know if she'll be willing to forgive what I did!'

'Whether she forgives you or not is entirely her prerogative but you owe it to her, and your own mental peace, to go and at least try. And you also need to take responsibility of your unborn child!'

Dushyant composed himself and said, 'You are right, Gurudev. I have to find her and seek her forgiveness.' A thought came into his head and he asked, 'Do you think Shakuntala really meant what she said about our child? Can a son ever fight his father for the throne?'

The kulguru was silent for a moment and then spoke thoughtfully, 'I have not seen or heard of that happening yet. But that doesn't imply it cannot happen in the future. Times are changing and the Tretayug has reached its zenith. Who knows what kind of abominations people in the coming ages might be capable of!'

'I hope such a time never comes, Gurudev,' Dushyant said despondently. 'What kind of society would we have if sons started killing their fathers or brothers for position or money? Imagine Shoor or Vasu plotting against me because they want the moon throne. It is incomprehensible!'

Dirghatamas shook his head sadly, 'The Asurs have given us a few examples already—Ravan threw his elder brother Kuber out of Lanka and usurped his kingdom. He was one of the major reasons why Kartavirya Arjun lost track of Dharma. I just hope these Asurik tendencies do not rise once again.'

The kulguru then turned to more pressing matters at hand, 'Before you head to Maharishi Kanav's ashram, we have to take care of the situation at the border. In the past month, despite your brothers' efforts, we have not achieved the desired results. I think it's time for you to step onto the battlefield. We have to crush this intrusion before the onset of winter.'

Dushyant was surprised at the news and asked, 'Why wasn't I made aware of this earlier, Gurudev?'

The acharya smiled and said, 'You were hardly present in any of the meetings, my king. Things were all right in the beginning and we seemed to be gaining the upper hand but lately there has been an influx of marauders from the north, especially the Shaks and the Hara-Huns. We have secured our western borders but the north still remains under threat. You should take the lead in crushing the barbarians and show your citizens that you can live up to the promise your father saw in you.'

The Puru king was ashamed to have let matters come to such a pass. He looked at the kulguru repentantly and said, 'Please request the council for an emergency meeting, Gurudev. I shall beg their forgiveness and discuss the strategy for this siege. I shall personally lead the charge against these Mlecchas and teach them a lesson they will never forget!'

Dirghatamas nodded and left the chambers with hope. Whether Shakuntala forgave Dushyant or not was a question for a later day, but at least the desire to meet her again would fuel his pupil's efforts to return victorious from the battle to save his kingdom.

Adhyaye 16

Shakuntala was back in the ashram by the banks of the Malini river.

Maharishi Kanav, who had divined the events of the past few days, had been ecstatic to see his chubby grandson. Weeping profusely, Shakuntala fell at his feet, letting out tears of shame and regret, but the Maharishi advised her to leave the past behind. The baby's arrival had brought a new hope into her life and she had to focus on the future now. He profusely thanked Menaka for coming to the aid of his adopted daughter and urged her to stay till the official naming ceremony of the child could be performed.

On the twelfth day of the child's birth, the ashram hermits gathered together to light the sacred yagnya fire and chant hymns to bless the child and give him a name. Before the ceremony began, Maharishi Kanav explained its significance to the assembled gathering, 'The first eleven post-natal days are considered crucial for the baby and the mother. Both of them pass through immense physical and emotional strain and require time to regain their health. After these eleven nights have passed, the naming ceremony can be performed.'

And then, he called on someone whom Shakuntala had never imagined she would see in her life. 'I request Brahmarishi Vishwamitra, the maternal grandfather of this blessed child, to come forward and perform the naamkaran ceremony.'

Both Shakuntala and Menaka were stunned. They couldn't believe their eyes when they saw the tall and impressively built Brahmarishi emerge from the crowd of hermits around them. Her heart brimming with conflicting emotions, Shakuntala looked at her birth father for the very first time in her life. Maharishi Kanav distracted her by pouring sanctified water in Shakuntala's right palm to wet the head of the baby in a symbol of purification. When she had done what was asked of her, Vishwamitra knelt in front of his daughter and asked, 'May I hold the baby?'

Shakuntala was too dazed by his sudden appearance to object. Taking the child in his arms Vishwamitra declared to the gathering, 'As the maternal grandfather of this radiant boy, I am honoured to be able to perform this ceremony to neutralize the sins, if any, of his past lives. I shall perform the rituals to ensure a glorious future for the baby with the utmost respect for etiquette and tradition.'

Menaka, in spite of her surprise, could not help but feel happy that the Brahmarishi was present for his grandchild's ceremony. Though her mind was swirling with hundreds of thoughts. This man was a far cry from the Vishwamitra she had known. That man had scoffed at tradition and taken pride in being blasphemous, whereas this Brahmarishi seemed to be a strict adherent of rituals and convention.

Shakuntala exchanged multiple looks with her mother, wondering how to deal with the reappearance of her father who seemed oblivious to their discomfort. As the yagnya fire was lit, Vishwamitra gave them both a genuine smile. Turning back to the gathering, he announced, 'I give the custody of this child to the moon, the sun, the guardians of the eight directions and the sky. May all the deities protect him by day and by night, whether the child is vigilant or not!'

Oblations were poured into the yagnya fire by the entire family and Maharishi Kanav explained the naming process. 'A boy's name should ideally consist of an even number of letters since Mahadev dominates those numbers while Devi dominates odd numbers. Since the child's mother wishes to keep a name with an odd number of letters, the child's life will be guided by Devi Shakti. I request the child's grandfather to whisper the name of the baby in his ears before announcing it to the world.'

As Vishwamitra brought the child closer, the sight of him filled his heart with a kind of love he had never experienced before. He whispered into the baby's ears the name he would be known by and shared it with the gathering, 'From this day onwards, this child shall be known as Sarvadaman, the subduer of all!'

Amidst sounds of 'Swasti' from the gathering, Maharishi Kanav gestured to Shakuntala to write the name with her finger in a plate of uncooked rice. Thereafter, he asked her to dip her finger in a small pot of honey and touch it to the baby's lips. Everyone rejoiced as the baby smacked his lips at the sweet taste. While the prasadam was being distributed to those present, Vishwamitra returned the child to his daughter with another bewildering smile and then sat down with Maharishi Kanav to prepare Sarvadaman's birth chart. As they plotted the planets and zodiacs based on the place and time of the birth of their grandson, they were amazed at the auspicious signs they could see in their analysis.

Maharishi Kanav remarked, 'This chart looks very promising, Brahmarishi.'

Marvelling at the conjunctions emerging out of the planetary positions, Vishwamitra nodded and replied,

'The presence of Mangal and Budh in Mesh rashi indicates Mahapurush Yog—he will be unmatched in valour and be brave and largely unconquerable. The presence of Brihaspati in Mithun confers Bhagya Yog or luck on him while the presence of Shani in Rishabh rashi gives him Khyati Yog. All the stars are aligned for Sarvadaman to become the king of this entire country some day!'

They looked at each other in amazement; such a horoscope could only have been matched by the birth chart of Kartavirya Arjun, the erstwhile emperor of the world. Vishwamitra could have visualized the entire future of the child had he wished to. But, what's the fun in that, he thought with a wry smile, let destiny play out however it wants. In the absence of the child's own father, he would be there to protect him.

Shakuntala was still recovering from the shock of seeing her father in the ceremony and leaving her son with Menaka, decided to confront Maharishi Kanav about Vishwamitra's presence. She stormed off to him and asked, 'Father, how could you invite the Brahmarishi to the ceremony?'

Kanav looked at Vishwamitra who was sitting beside him, and replied, 'My dear child, the Brahmarishi arrived this morning to seek my permission to attend the ceremony. I could not refuse him in all good conscience. He is your birth father after all and his blessings can only help Sarvadaman in the future.'

Shakuntala knew she couldn't really blame the Maharishi for his decision; he had had Sarvadaman's best interests in mind. But she was not ready to accept Vishwamitra in her life just yet. As she turned to the Brahmarishi, her eyes burning in anger, Maharishi Kanav silently walked away to give them an opportunity to talk in private. A sudden hush fell around father and daughter, punctuated only by the rustling of leaves.

Vishwamitra looked at the enraged young woman in front of him and said calmly, 'Before you say anything, I wish to apologize for my absence in your life until now. My role in your life was destined to begin at this juncture and I am here, ready to take on the responsibility.'

Shakuntala's anger erupted at his words and all the resentment she had felt for him growing up burst out of her in one angry question. 'Who gave you permission to decide when you could enter my life, Brahmarishi? What right do you have to come barging in here now, after neglecting your responsibilities for two decades?'

'I came here to see you and bless your son. I am a sanyasi now, with no family ties, but I had to meet you once to explain why I was absent for such a long time. You may think I was punishing you for your mother's actions but the thought never crossed my mind. You were born after she left my ashram and by the time I learnt of your birth, you had already been adopted by Maharishi Kanav. I wanted to come and take you with me but realized that my mind was consumed by my desire for revenge. In Maharishi Kanav's care, you would have received the love that I could not provide in that mental state. For the betterment of your future, I decided to disappear into the shadows.'

Shakuntala felt like screaming. Instead she said, 'How could you decide what is best for me without even giving me a glance? You thought I would live happily in my ignorance and you would be absolved of your duties?'

'No, my dear,' Vishwamitra explained patiently, 'I was in constant touch with Maharishi Kanav regarding your growth and development. I have cared more for you than I did for your brother Deval; he hasn't even seen me since I left Kanyakubja.'

'Didn't you adopt that Brahmin child you rescued in Ayodhya?' Shakuntala asked caustically, 'How could you adopt another child while forsaking your own biological children?' The acid in her voice was strong enough to burn her father's stoic façade.

'Devrat needed me Shakuntala. His own father sold him so that Harishchandra could sacrifice his life to save that of the prince. It was a ceremony that made my guru leave Ayodhya and compelled me to take over his responsibilities for the sake of bringing justice to this world. I had to step in to save the life of that little boy and restore his trust in humanity! As far as you are concerned, it was only the knowledge that you would have a better home with the Maharishi that made me stay away from you. Maharishi Kanav was childless and I knew he would leave no stone unturned in raising you as his own daughter. Neither Menaka nor I were capable of providing you the warmth of a stable household. Under the circumstances staying away was the best thing we could have done for you.'

Shakuntala suddenly felt drained of the desire to fight. On one hand was the resentment she harboured for this man and on the other was the possibility of finally getting closure and freedom from the self-doubt that had plagued her all through her adult life. Maybe the Brahmarishi was telling the truth; just like her mother, he too had no selfish motive to come back into her life. They had both returned because they cared for her welfare, at a time when she needed people to lean on for moral support. She could choose to stay bitter about her parents' absence and keep the fire of hatred burning inside her heart. Or, she could let go of her anger and forgive them for their follies. She would wait and see how things turned out in the future. Perhaps Vishwamitra could help her exact the revenge that she desperately wanted.

Adhyaye 17

Dushyant returned to Hastinapur after three months of fighting at the borders of his kingdom. The battles along the northern frontiers of the Puru kingdom were successful in keeping the barbarians at bay for the time being but there was no way to know how long the peace would last. Before some new political exigency occurred, he set about making preparations to visit Maharishi Kanav's ashram. The original plan had been to take a huge procession to welcome Shakuntala in a manner befitting the queen of the kingdom, but Acharya Dirghatamas tactfully advised the king against it; he did not want Dushyant to be shamed in front of everyone in case the girl refused to come with him.

Suggesting an alternative plan he said, 'Why don't we position the royal cavalcade at the edge of the forest while you go to the ashram by yourself just like the first time?'

'How will that help, Gurudev?' Dushyant asked.

'Since you could not gain Maharishi Kanav's audience the last time you were in his hermitage it seems prudent to do so now. It will give you the opportunity to seek his permission to speak with Shakuntala instead of arriving at his doorstep unannounced with a royal entourage. That way, it will neither disturb the forest dwellers too much nor paint a sorry picture for us in case Shakuntala doesn't come back with you immediately.'

Dirghatamas was careful not to mention a complete negation of the possibility of her return but Dushyant understood the implication of his words anyway and submitted to his logic. The king was prepared for Shakuntala's refusal but he was determined to do everything the right way this time.

Within a week, a grand procession of royally decked elephants, horses and chariots carrying the king and his cavalcade set off for the woods. Although the ostensible reason given was that the king and his brothers were going to the forest to relax after the months spent in war, Dushyant had opened up to his brothers and shared the plan with them. He was glad for their support as well as the kulguru's guidance and his heart filled with hope as he returned to the place where the story had begun. He had met Shakuntala while wandering alone in the forest; he would meet her again in the same circumstances and try to rekindle the magic between them.

He asked his brothers to wait at the same spot where they had rested all those months ago while he set out on his own. As he led his horse towards the bamboo grove, he was reminded of how he had made a complete fool of himself, rushing out with a spear in his hand, trying to save Shakuntala from her own pet. His laughter was soon replaced by a stinging in his eyes. He had made a complete mess of their relationship and his heart ached to see her again and beg for her forgiveness.

Riding eastward through the undergrowth in a slow canter, he would have reached the ashram in no time had he not chanced upon an incredible sight. A magnificent lioness was resting in a patch of sunlit grass with her cubs frolicking around her. And on her back sat a human child! Dushyant let out an involuntary gasp.

The sound made the animal rise and look at him with keen eyes. Dushyant reined in his horse and assessed the situation. The creature's movement had caused the small child on its back to flop down onto the soft grass. Fair and chubby with a mop of curly dark hair, the boy seemed oblivious to the danger that the beast posed and was now rolling about with one of the cubs. Dushyant observed the scene unfold with a sense of déjà vu and concluded that the animal must belong to Maharishi Kanav's ashram. He was surprised that the usually protective lioness was letting the boy play with her cubs as if he was a part of the pack. Even as he watched in fascination, the child grabbed the cub closest to him and opened its mouth to count its teeth!

There was a movement in the woods in front of him and the toddler immediately turned in that direction and exclaimed in his gibberish, 'Ma, lion-baby teeth!'

Dushyant hid behind a nearby tree to see who the mother of this brave child was. The moment the lady stepped into the sunlight, his breath caught in his throat. Shakuntala! He had prepared himself to greet the Maharishi first and gauge his reaction before meeting his daughter but it seemed that fate was conspiring to bring them face-to-face once again.

Shakuntala's attention was focused on her son and she shouted, 'Daman, leave the cub and come to me, it is time for supper.'

'No, Ma . . . teeth!' the child replied, urging her to come and see for herself what he had just discovered.

Shakuntala smiled at his exuberance. 'You can do that some other time, my love, the lioness is not going anywhere.'

As she took a few steps towards her son, she noticed the man on the horse amidst the trees.

Dushyant waited for as long as he could for his heartbeat to steady and dismounted from his steed. As he stepped out of the shadows Shakuntala gasped in surprise and froze as if she had been hit by lightning.

Dushyant addressed her in a voice full of contrition, 'I can't believe I am seeing you again.'

The sound of his voice broke the spell Shakuntala was under. She ran towards the animal and scooped up her son into her arms while the lioness scampered away with her cubs. The animal's departure galvanized Dushyant into action and he rushed forward.

'Shakuntala!' he cried out in anguish. 'Forgive me! I will face all the censure you have in store for me, but please, do not go away without listening to what I have to say.'

'I do not wish to speak with you, *King* Dushyant,' Shakuntala said in a trembling voice. She would not allow herself to be seduced by his clever words again.

The child looked at them curiously, wondering who the man was who had upset his mother. Seeing how distraught she was and how terrified of his presence the boy seemed, a feeling of acute regret overpowered Dushyant. *How could he have done this to his beautiful family?*

'How can I leave you now after spending months waiting to meet you again?'

Shakuntala responded in a voice that dripped of sarcasm, 'What made you wait? You knew very well that the only place I could go to after the way you humiliated me in your court was my father's ashram. If you had wanted to apologize you could have come here sooner!'

'I wanted to, Shakuntala, believe me!' Dushyant pleaded. 'But even before your arrival there was trouble brewing at my kingdom's borders and after you left, the situation became too urgent to ignore! I have spent the last three months fighting multiple battles with various enemies, and it was only the desire to see you again that helped me survive the ordeal!'

Shakuntala was silent. Lately, with so many of her family members rediscovering their love for her, it had become difficult for her to sift the truth from the lies. While she could give her parents the benefit of the doubt, she could not forget that Dushyant had berated and insulted her in his court like no woman should ever be.

As memories of that fateful day resurfaced she suppressed the urge to lash out at him and said calmly, 'Be that as it may, I do not wish to have anything to do with your lies any more.'

Dushyant knew he would never get the opportunity to atone for his actions again so he knelt before her and said earnestly, 'Shakuntala, I beg you! No lies, no deceptions. Please just give me one chance to explain.'

Shakuntala stopped trying to move away and gave in to his request. She deserved to know the reason for his actions that day. And if she were honest, a part of her was glad to see him grovelling at her feet.

Dushyant breathed a sigh of relief and stood up. 'I had left the forest determined to secure my father's permission to bring you to Hastinapur but when I reached home, instead of his warm embrace, I found his lifeless body lying in the royal hall.'

He shook his head to banish the images of his father's body being consumed by fire and said, 'I felt guilty for not returning earlier and, in my frustration, blamed our relationship for the delay. I know it was foolish and childish, but I could not rid myself of the shame and avoided calling you to the capital. Perhaps, in time I would have, but then you arrived unannounced in the court and I was so taken aback by your sudden appearance that I ended up doing something completely unforgivable and dastardly.'

Shakuntala saw the look of extreme sadness on his face and said, 'You know, Dushyant, choosing you as my husband and travelling to Hastinapur to meet you—both of these were decisions I had taken by myself. You broke my confidence in one stroke with your unwarranted cruelty. You took the easy way out by not dealing with the situation and made me suffer the consequences!'

'I am deeply aware and regretful of the hurt I caused you,' Dushyant said plaintively. 'Believe me, I have suffered as much in my regret as you have in your anger.'

Shakuntala shook her head, refusing to accept his apology. She countered, 'The Shastras proclaim a wife to be a man's better half, the first of friends. She is the root of religion as well as salvation. No householder can perform religious acts without having his wife by his side. Yet you scorned me like a cheap courtesan and threw me out like a used piece of cloth!' Hot tears of anger and grief escaped her eyes and, sensing his mother's distress, the child in her arms also began to cry. 'You not only insulted your wife but also your unborn child. From the tiniest to the largest, all creatures protect their young, even lay down their lives for them, but you, the mighty king of Hastinapur, had no compassion for this child who was growing in my womb. How can I forget the feeling of utter desolation that your actions caused me?'

'I was self-centred, Shakuntala,' Dushyant admitted, bowing his head. 'But do consider that even though I refused to accept you on that fateful day, I have not said yes to any of the multiple proposals that my coronation brought with it. In my heart I knew I had to seek you out again.'

Shakuntala was affected by the last sentence. She stood quietly, trying to calm both her son as well as the turmoil raging in her mind. As Sarvadaman's sobs subsided, she looked pointedly at Dushyant and said, 'The shock of your desertion and my public humiliation triggered the premature birth of your son. It is only due to the same parents whom you had abused in court that he is alive now. I believe the best punishment for you would be to keep you away from him!'

Dushyant fell to his knees again and said mournfully, 'I have no words to atone for the ones I had uttered earlier! But I can only say this: You promised to make me bow before my son one day. Here I am, kneeling in front of both of you, pleading for your mercy. Isn't this what you wished for? Isn't this a defeat of sorts? We have the chance to end this misery right now, Shakuntala. Let me take you back to the palace where you belong.'

Shakuntala's mind went back to the story her mother had told her about the daughter of Indra's charioteer. Her desire for revenge would exact an unfair struggle from Sarvadaman. Dushyant was contrite and remorseful. Would she be justified in subjecting her son to the hardships of the jungle when he could have the moon throne this instant?

She looked at her son's cherubic face that resembled his father's in so many ways and suddenly she knew what she had to do. Taking Sarvadaman's tiny hand she put it in Dushyant's and said in a voice filled with emotion, 'Daman, meet your father.'

Adhyaye 18

Dushyant shuddered with nervous apprehension as he finally brought his family into Hastinapur the way he should have many months ago. After Shakuntala had accepted his apology, he had rushed to beg Maharishi Kanav's forgiveness and seek his permission to take Sarvadaman and Shakuntala with him.

As the grand procession of royally decked elephants, horses and chariots carrying the king and his family proceeded towards Hastinapur, Sarvadaman looked about him with excitement. This was the first time he was being taken out of the forest. He was barely a few months old, yet his body already looked like that of a two-year-old. Dushyant had been amazed as well as a little alarmed at his son's rapid development but Vishwamitra assured him that the pace of the child's growth would slow down with age.

All of Hastinapur was decorated with flowers in honour of their return, and as the royal family passed through the massive city gates, they were showered with flower petals by the elated citizens. There was an air of celebration with people rejoicing and dancing all through the streets. It seemed as if the entire city had come out to greet their queen and the young prince. At the palace steps, the king and his family were greeted by

Dushyant's brothers' wives, who stood with aarti thalis, lamps and garlands in their hands. Acharya Dirghatamas blessed the royal family with holy water and uttered some Vedic chants before stepping aside to let them enter the royal hall.

Shakuntala was so overwhelmed with the grand reception that she could not hold back her tears. This was the sort of welcome she had wished for when she had come to Hastinapur for the very first time. Knowing that it was a momentous occasion for her, Menaka and Vishwamitra followed at a discrete distance, allowing her to bask in the attention. Over the past few months, they had become more cordial to each other and both were glad that they could move past their broken relationship as mature adults.

Dushyant walked up the steps leading to the moon throne with his wife and son, and the three stood with folded hands, bowing to the assembled gathering. A loud roar of approval rose from the citizens gathered in the royal hall. Raising his hands to quieten the crowd, the king said, 'My dear citizens of Hastinapur, I thank you for the blessings you all have showered on me and my family.'

He had to publicly undo the wrongs he had committed earlier so he declared in a loud voice, 'I have let my wife and son stay away from me, and all of you, for far too long. Due to unfounded apprehensions, I did them a grave injustice but from this day forth, everything changes. I hereby declare my wife Shakuntala the queen of Hastinapur, and our son Sarvadaman my heir.'

Sounds of 'Swasti' echoed throughout the hall, wishing auspiciousness for the family, as the three took their seats on the throne. Dushyant was glad that his subjects had accepted Shakuntala and Sarvadaman with an open heart.

He exchanged a look with his father-in-law and on receiving a confirmatory nod, made another announcement, 'I have requested Brahmarishi Vishwamitra to remain here for Prince Sarvadaman's guidance and he has graciously agreed. May the future of Puruvansh be secured forever with the blessings of the man who discovered the mighty Gayatri Mantra!'

Vishwamitra came forward to bless the assembly and declared, 'Destiny works in mysterious ways, even for Brahmarishis. I had quit the material trappings of this world many years ago when I left Kanyakubja, but within just two decades, I am back where I began. I will be here for the guidance of the future king of Puruvansh!'

He looked at his grandson who sat contentedly between his parents and said, 'I don't know whether his name is a cause or effect, but Sarvadaman was truly the subduer of all in Maharishi Kanav's ashram. This boy is like a flame which, when it grows, will surely turn into a roaring fire. The wheels of his chariot shall cross the length and the breadth of this great country and he shall bring great glory to the clan of Puru Chandravanshis.'

At these words the entire assembly was filled with a hope for better times. As Vishwamitra came back to his seat, the crowd cheered lustily, 'Long live Maharaj Dushyant! Long live Maharani Shakuntala! Long live Yuvraj Sarvadaman!'

It was Kulguru Dirghatamas's turn to address the gathering. 'There is no greater blessing in one's life than the presence of a learned guru. I do not say this because I consider myself a great and wise sage'—the crowd tittered politely at his self-deprecating words—'but to stress upon Hastinapur's good fortune in having the erudite and accomplished Brahmarishi Vishwamitra here among us. All Chandravanshis know that the lunar dynasty originated with the birth of our Lord Chandrama to Brahma's son Atri and his chaste wife Anasuya. But there is one aspect of the story that you may not be aware of and with the indulgence of our kind king, I would like to share it with you.'

The acharya looked at Dushyant who folded his hands and urged him to continue.

Nodding, the kulguru began, 'We think of Lord Chandrama as a mighty warrior and benevolent king, but did you know, that there was a very real danger of him not surviving after his birth past a few minutes?'

The gathering fell silent for no one had heard of this before. 'Let me enlighten you with the legends in this regard. When that great being was born he was so cold that his parents could not bear his touch for more than a moment. Then the Ashta-dikpals, the guardians of the eight directions, arrived to help Maharishi Atri but even they could not hold him for too long, passing him from one to other. During the exchange, the boy slipped out of their hands and fell on the floor!'

There was a collective gasp from the audience. Shakuntala wrapped a protective arm around her son. She could not imagine any kind of mishap befalling her beloved son and sympathized with what Chandrama's parents must have gone through.

Acharya Dirghatamas continued, 'When even the Ashta-dikpals couldn't handle the child, the creator of the universe, Srishti-Karta Brahma himself appeared with his other Manas Putras, who were the boy's uncles. It was these accomplished sages—Angiras, Bhrigu, Pulah, Pulatsya and others—who took the child in their arms and assumed the responsibility of his upbringing. And it was only because of the knowledge received from these great rishis that our Lord Chandrama became the lord of the moon from where he makes all the eight directions glow with the moonshine.'

At the end of his story the kulguru turned to Vishwamitra with folded hands and said, 'I hope the Brahmarishi, who has even greater achievements to his name than the sons of Brahma, will help our Yuvraj achieve even loftier heights than his illustrious forefather.'

There was loud applause as the kulguru took his seat and Vishwamitra bowed to the senior rishi with all sincerity. Almost everyone in Nabhi-varsh knew about his exemplary achievements, and they hoped that his presence would help the Purus advance in their spiritual sojourn just as the Suryavanshis had done under the able guidance of Brahmarishi Vasishth.

It was the beginning of a new era for Hastinapur.

Adhyaye 19

In the coming weeks, as she watched Sarvadaman grow in the luxury of the palace, Shakuntala was glad about the decisions she had taken. Things had truly begun to change for the better. Sarvadaman was five now, and the Brahmarishi had decided to start his formal education in the same way he had been trained by Rishi Dattatreya.

As the boy came running on his pudgy feet for his first lesson, Vishwamitra said with a barely suppressed smile. 'Your mother worries that you spend too much time fighting with other boys. Perhaps you should start devoting more time to learning a bit about the scriptures with this old man.'

Sarvadaman gave him a roguish smile and said innocently, 'But I don't fight with anyone, Pitamah. If they tease me and call me a small boy, I just show them that I am not smaller than them.'

His grandfather finally gave in to his urge to smile and said, 'Well, you *are* a small boy even if you don't look like one! It is good to not let anyone bully you but you have to ensure you don't become a bully yourself. Our true strength lies in learning from our experiences. We shall commence our lesson with a few examples from our surroundings. Are you ready?'

Sarvadaman nodded eagerly, remembering what his mother had said to him a few days ago. He was lucky to have a Brahmarishi as his teacher; not many could boast of that distinction and he would do well to imbibe all the knowledge that Vishwamitra had to share.

His guru started the lesson, 'We begin today with the ten gurus of nature. The very first of these is Prithvi, our mother earth. Can you think of something that we could learn from her?'

'Is it generosity?' the young prince asked, surprising his grandfather with his reply.

'Excellent! We should indeed learn how to serve selflessly, but there is also another lesson to be imbibed from Bhumi Devi, the goddess of the earth, and that is developing infinite patience. No matter how we explore her resources—digging, mining, ploughing, prodding—she bears the pain with patience, sharing her bounty when we have toiled hard enough to know its value. So along with her munificence, we also have to learn the art of endurance from her.'

The child noted down the two points diligently on his palmyra leaf and then looked at his guru expectantly.

Vishwamitra continued with the lesson. 'Our next teacher is Varun Deva, who governs the precious resource of water. Water can clean anything just by its touch and we should strive to emulate that quality so that even if we come in contact with unscrupulous souls, the purity of our heart remains unaffected.'

Sarvadaman had barely noted the quality of purity when his guru said, 'Our third teacher is Vayu, the wind god. Wind moves through mountains, streams, deserts and valleys with the same impartiality. We should also go through life without developing any biases or affection, for in the end we all have to leave this world alone.'

The thought was confusing to the young child and he asked, 'Should I not even be attached to you?'

The Brahmarishi understood his feelings and replied, 'Of course you should! After all family is the first and basic unit in the building of any society. But your attachment should not keep you from finding your own destiny. Our obligations to friends, elders, family and society have to be fulfilled, but in a dispassionate manner. When people fail to do so, they end up favouring their own kith and kin at the expense of other more deserving candidates. A king, being the final decision-maker in any kingdom, can never be partial.'

The train of thought led the boy to another question. 'Then why does a king not select the most capable person from his kingdom to be his successor? Why is it that only a king's son or daughter can sit on the throne?'

Vishwamitra was impressed with the child's intuitive reasoning and he replied with candour, 'Because even though this is the ideal way to select a ruler of the land, it is practically impossible to be completely fair in it as well! There are many tribes in our country that elect their own representatives, but as the size of the kingdom grows, it becomes more and more difficult to ensure that the people, while making their choice, are not swayed by their own attachments to clan, tribe, region and the like.

'It takes a certain kind of leader—strong and charismatic— to bring citizens from different parts of a kingdom together, and such kings are few and far between. Our best option is to train princes and princesses from a very young age to make them capable of running a kingdom so that when the time comes, the king can choose one who is worthy to sit on the throne. Also, there are a definite set of rules that the monarch has to abide by and bodies like the royal council that can impose checks and balances on his unlimited powers.'

While Sarvadaman made notes, the Brahmarishi continued, 'The fourth teacher is Agni Deva, the god of fire, who not only provides heat but also light. Just as fire burns itself to give light to others, we too should burn our own ego through knowledge and share the flame of enlightenment with those around us.'

'The fifth guru is Dyaus, the ruler of the sky above, who shelters us from the fiery bodies of the solar system. He absorbs the impact of each meteor and asteroid that blazes through the heavens, saving life on this planet from complete extinction. As soldiers of Dharma, we should be strong enough to combat Asurik powers and defend those under our protection.'

The prince's curiosity was piqued by the image of celestial bodies bombarding earth and he asked excitedly, 'Why don't we see these blazing heavenly rocks, Pitamah? Is it because the sky god is such a good guardian?'

Vishwamitra nodded. 'It is difficult to spot them during the day in sunlight but sometimes, when the impact is massive, they appear as meteor showers in the night. Very rarely does a huge rock get past the protection of the sky to make it noticeable even in daytime. It happened millions of years ago, when giant lizards were wiped off our planet, but such impacts are few and far in between. This also shows that if we fail to protect the ones we are supposed to, how deeply it can impact their lives.'

'The above five are the Panch Mahabhoot, the building blocks of life. Now for the sixth guru: Surya, the sun god.

Surya not only supports the nine planets through the power of samkarshan but is also the primary source of the energy that allows life to thrive on the earth. We should strive to be like the sun, passing on positive energy to everyone around us.'

He paused for a moment to gauge if Sarvadaman had understood the importance of his words. Satisfied with his observation, he moved on. 'You love playing with the lion cubs that you asked your father to bring with you from the forest, so the next four teachers I am going to talk about are the beasts of the jungle. Can you guess the first one?'

Sarvadaman replied excitedly, 'I am sure it is the lion! He is the king of the jungle so we should all be brave like him.'

'You are right about the lion's bravery. How about the honey bee?'

'The bee?' Sarvadaman asked in surprise. 'What can the tiny stinging bee teach us?'

Vishwamitra laughed at his grandson's expression. 'The size, colour, beauty, gender or race of a being is no consideration while choosing a teacher. Bees spend hours gathering honey from flowers spread far and wide, and it is we humans who take advantage of their hard work. There are two important lessons to be learnt from them—first, we should not limit ourselves while gathering knowledge and should be willing to go where the path takes us, and second, it is useless to hoard things, for one day, they shall pass on to someone else!

'Our next guru is the elephant but not for the reason that you might suspect. Yes, it is a strong animal, but it also has a fabulous memory. These lumbering tuskers do not forget incidents for a long time; nor should we forget the lessons learnt during our life.'

Subtly, the Brahmarishi was introducing the concept of kingship to his grandson. 'The ninth teacher is the fish that is easily trapped by the fisherman's bait. We should learn to eschew greed, lest we fall in someone's trap and lose our independence. This is especially important for a king who may be lured by those seeking to fulfil their own ulterior motives.

'Our last guru is the caterpillar, which goes through multiple stages of development to emerge as the beautiful butterfly. Like it, we should evolve continually, eventually letting go of the outer sheath of our body, so that in the end our soul can free itself from the fetters of material bondage and attain nirvana.'

Adhyaye 20

Dushyant was glad his son's training was going well. The Brahmarishi was sowing the seeds of Dharma early on and the king appreciated his efforts. Many great leaders and kings of the world had lost direction and ended up on the wrong side of Dharma, rendering all their achievements futile.

But it took more than scriptural knowledge to mould a prince into a good king, and more than anything, his son would need reliable allies. Dushyant's own marriage to Shakuntala had opened up a new vista of cooperation with Mahodayapur, the erstwhile kingdom of Brahmarishi Vishwamitra. King Deval had already visited his stepsister in her new home a few times. This alliance had strengthened Puru's southern borders but Dushyant wanted Sarvadaman to have a support system beyond family.

The perfect opportunity to secure such support presented itself a few years later when they received an invitation from Ayodhya for the coronation of Rohitashwa, the son of King Harishchandra. Dushyant decided to send Vishwamitra and Sarvadaman as representatives of the kingdom of Puru, along with a platoon of soldiers, elephants and horse-carts laden with precious jewels and other valuable gifts for the new king.

In Ayodhya, Vishwamitra and Sarvadaman were greeted by King Harishchandra, Queen Taramati and Prince Rohitashwa, who respectfully ushered them into the palace. Sarvadaman marvelled at the grandeur of the sandstone and pink marble palace that was seven storeys tall. Intricately carved pillars held up a massive ceiling depicting the exploits of the sun god and his brothers. The powerful presence of the twelve solar gods filled the circular hall. The Suryavanshi throne was similar to the moon throne, shaped like the cosmic chariot of Surya with seven steeds replacing the antelopes of Hastinapur.

Harishchandra was ageing well and Vishwamitra was glad to see him in good health. He was even more pleased to meet his mentor and guide Brahmarishi Vasishth who had resumed his role as the kulguru of Kosal. He greeted the venerable sage with folded hands and the elderly rishi invited them to sit beside him.

'I can't believe I am in the presence of not one but two Brahmarishis!' Harishchandra said once everyone had settled down. 'I must be the most fortunate king in all of Nabhi-varsh to have received blessings from both Gurudev Vasishth as well as Brahmarishi Vishwamitra.'

While Vasishth gave an approving nod, Vishwamitra responded more deferentially, 'The honour is mine to be seated in this august assembly once again. I have been hearing great things about your reign, my king, and I congratulate you on remaining true to the promise you made to me. I am sure Guru Vasishth's return from the Himalayas has helped you grow spiritually as well.'

Sarvadaman appraised the senior Brahmarishi critically and wondered what he had done to command such respect.

Vasishth was tall and impressive but to him he looked like any other aged rishi. His long snow-white hair was kept in place by a string of rudraksh while tulsi beads adorned his neck. His eyes had the fieriness of molten lava and he wore saffron garments and the mark of a Vaishnav on his forehead.

The king bowed his head in acknowledgement and replied, 'The promise I made to you shall be my guiding force till my last breath, Brahmarishi. Some people have taken to calling me Satyavadi Harishchandra for following the principles of Dharma even during the most adverse conditions but I have been able to do so only because of your teachings!'

Vishwamitra replied with a smile, 'You have earned their respect as any good king should, Maharaj. Speaking of kingship, I must congratulate Rohitashwa for the upcoming coronation.' Turning to the prince he said, 'You must be a really accomplished young man to receive the blessings of my guru, Vasishth!'

The prince folded his hands humbly in a gesture of thankfulness. He had inherited the pleasant personality of his father and the sharp features of his mother.

Brahmarishi Vasishth nodded in approval and said, 'Prince Rohitashwa is more than capable and, if I might add, quite eager to discharge his duties as the next king but I wanted to wait for Parshu-Raam to finish his campaign in our neighbouring countries so that matters become more stable politically.'

'I understand, Gurudev. Raam's mission while necessary is also extremely unsettling. Now that his battle has moved to the other side of the globe, you believe the time is right for the young prince to take over.'

The elder Brahmarishi nodded. Then, sighing deeply, he said, 'Vishwamitra, your grand-nephew has taken an enormous burden on his shoulders. Sometimes when I am in deep meditation, I hear the blood-curdling screams of his victims as they are pushed into oblivion by his divine axe. All this carnage and destruction, even though necessary, is bound to leave some scars on his psyche. You must help him heal when he finally returns.'

Vishwamitra responded in a solemn tone, 'Gurudev, Raam shall abide by the difficult decisions he has taken in life, but I shall keep your advice in mind and help him in any way I can.'

As the discussion moved towards more serious matters of state, the crown prince of Ayodhya politely asked Sarvadaman if he would like to step out and talk in a less formal setting. The two young men took the elders' permission and walked out into the garden, followed discretely by a few guards. The fragrance of wild roses hung in the air, mingling with sweet birdsong as they strolled around the multiple fountains.

Prior to this, Sarvadaman had never met another crown prince apart from his uncle Deval's son from Kanyakubja, but he felt completely at ease with Rohitashwa. He was also glad for the chance to talk to him alone since there were many queries bubbling in his mind that the older prince could help him with. They stopped to sit on a bench and he finally asked the questions burning in his mind, 'Bhrata Rohit, would you mind if I ask you a few details about Brahmarishi Vasishth?'

Rohitashwa looked at him with an amused expression and said, 'Not at all. What is it that has piqued your curiosity about our kulguru?'

Sarvadaman grinned sheepishly. 'I was just wondering why my grandfather respects him so much. I know Guru Vasishth is the son of Srishti-Karta Brahma, but surely that can't be the only reason. They are both Brahmarishis of equal stature, yet, I have never seen Pitamah behave so respectfully with anyone else.'

'Surely Brahmarishi Vishwamitra must have told you something about his guru?'

Sarvadaman shook his head, 'To be honest, I have never really thought of asking any of my elders about their earlier lives. Between the three of them, they keep me quite busy what with martial training and scriptural discourses. The thought of finding out more about them never really crossed my mind!'

The crown prince of Ayodhya looked at Sarvadaman thoughtfully and said, 'I understand. We tend to take our families and what they do for us for granted. As a child I witnessed my own parents undergoing tremendous hardships for me but it was only years later that I truly realized the gravity of their situation. And by the way, since you do not know his history, it was your grandfather who had put them through all that.'

'What!' Sarvadaman exclaimed in surprise. He could not believe that his beloved pitamah could have intentionally caused anyone misery. Clearly, there was a lot he did not know about his own family. He looked at Rohitashwa, expecting to see signs of anger on his face but the prince seemed to have shared the information without any malice.

Rohitashwa smiled at Sarvadaman's confused expressions. 'It was done for the betterment of Kosal and my parents understand that. It is customary for great rishis to test their followers' dedication to Dharma with tough tasks. Your grandfather not only saved us from committing a heinous crime but also protected the life of the boy Devrat who takes care of his ashram in Naimish Aranya.

'But I digress. You wanted to know why your Pitamah respects our kulguru so much. This goes back to the time when Brahmarishi Vishwamitra was a king. He was ambitious and soon began annexing other kingdoms to expand his frontiers. While returning from one of these conquests, he encountered Brahmarishi Vasishth. That chance meeting inspired him to leave everything and become an ascetic. Thereafter he discovered the Gayatri Mantra, and even challenged the mighty Indra to attain the title of Brahmarishi! You should ask your Pitamah about his past. His life is a shining example of what an ordinary human being can achieve once he sets his heart to it.'

Sarvadaman nodded in understanding, his respect for his guru and grandfather deepening. He resolved to learn more about his exemplary life and make him proud of his grandson.

Sarvadaman

Adhyaye 21

The years were passing quickly and Sarvadaman was turning into a handsome young man. He had his father's unruly mop of hair and brown eyes but his complexion was flawless like that of his mother. His straight, slightly upturned nose and high cheekbones, combined with the first flush of youth, gave him an aura of invincible nobility.

Dushyant had left no stone unturned in grooming his son for his future role as king of Hastinapur. Along with the knowledge of the scriptures that he acquired from his grandfather, the prince was training under the ablest of Puru generals, learning and mastering various forms of martial combat as well as yogic exercises that enabled him to survive without food or water for a long time. Already an expert swordsman and master in fighting with the mace—contests of brute strength and strategy—he had now decided to turn his attention to archery. The sight of multiple archers practicing on different targets in the arena sent adrenaline coursing through his body. The only sounds he heard were the *twang* of bowstrings and the *whoosh* of arrows as they sliced through the air to unerringly hit their targets.

Noticing his rapt expression, Vishwamitra, who had accompanied him, said, 'At first glance, shooting an arrow looks like child's play. You take a bow in your hands, nock the arrow on the bowstring, draw, take aim and launch it with a flourish. Yes, all this is simple enough, but what *is* difficult is making sure that the arrow hits its target.'

Sarvadaman nodded in understanding.

Vishwamitra continued, 'There are various forces acting on an arrow during its launch and subsequent flight, and a good archer needs to keep them in mind for accuracy. The principles are roughly the same for any bowman, but some of the details vary depending upon a person's body type, size and strength. The best archers make shooting an arrow seem effortless because they are focused on the movement.'

He took Sarvadaman to a corner where unused bows of various sizes were hung and asked him to choose one according to his size. The prince selected a bow that was almost as tall as he was. The Brahmarishi nodded in appreciation, 'You have chosen the longbow favoured by many great archers. Even Lord Shiva is believed to use the longbow on occasion instead of the trident.'

Sarvadaman was thrilled to hear that but his grandfather cautioned him against being too pleased. 'Merely choosing the right weapon is not enough. You must learn how to use it properly. Besides learning the correct technique, you also need to develop the physical strength to wield it.'

Pointing to his pupil's back, arm and shoulders, the guru said, 'The trapezius, the triceps, and the deltoids are the strong muscles of back, arm and shoulders respectively. When combined with correct bone alignment, these give the strength to shoot consistently without tiring yourself out.

The further you draw the bowstring and the greater the force with which you do it, the greater is the energy with which the arrow is shot.'

Next, Vishwamitra taught him how to string a bow and the importance of using the correct material. 'The string should be light, yet strong and resistant to wear and tear. Any naturally occurring fibre can be used, including linen, hemp, vegetable fibres, silk or even animal sinew.'

Sarvadaman was increasingly becoming enamoured by the intricate details of the art. He listened to his grandfather with complete attention as he instructed him about the correct stance. 'You must have a consistent anchor point when drawing the string. Do you want to try a few postures to find one that suits you?'

The prince nodded eagerly and copied his grandfather's stance.

'For a novice,' Vishwamitra continued, 'what's more important than hitting the target is learning to shoot in a straight line. This can be done by bringing the elbow on your string arm to the same point each time. If you are consistent in the way you shoot, there's no doubt that you will get better with each shot.'

They worked on a few different stances to help Sarvadaman settle on the one he was most comfortable with. He observed the other archers practicing in the arena and took cues from them as well.

Sarvadaman's mind was bursting with questions and he asked, 'Pitamah, you mentioned that Lord Shiva uses a longbow. Does any other deity? I know Indra uses the Vajra and Varun is fond of his cosmic noose but are there any other archers in the pantheon?'

The Brahmarishi thought for a moment and replied, 'Well, Shiva's longbow, known as Pinak, is actually a counterpart of Sharang, the bow Vishwakarma crafted for Lord Vishnu. Both of them have used their bows on various occasions but there are a few popular stories about them that I can tell you if you want.'

'Please do!' Sarvadaman said excitedly, as he was fond of listening to the Puranic tales of gods and demons. His grandmother had kept him entertained with them throughout his childhood and he secretly wished to be remembered like them some day as the champion of the righteous.

'Do you know why we celebrate the festival of Dev-Deepawali on the night of Kartik Purnima?'

The prince shook his head so his grandfather continued, 'There was once an Asur named Tarak who wished to rule the three worlds. He had terrorized the Devas in the higher Lokas and the humans on Prithvi. Tarak was finally slain by Shiva's son Kartikeya. The demon's three sons—Tarakaksh, Kamalaksh and Vidyunmali—fled from their own planet when Kartikeya's troops attacked and found refuge on its three satellites.

'After a long and difficult tapasya, they obtained the boon of invincibility from Srishti-Karta Brahma, but it would only hold true as long as they did not appear together in the same spatial co-ordinates. This boon spurred the three into avenging their father's death. They mounted swift attacks on their enemies and returned to their individual cities before any action could be taken against them. Knowing that the brothers would never gather in one place if they could help it, Shiva decided to target them when the three satellites aligned in a straight line during the course of their natural revolution.'

Vishwamitra was narrating the events of those bygone ages as if he could see the moment in his mind. Sarvadaman wasn't surprised. He knew his grandfather could see everything that had happened in the past, present and future anywhere in the three worlds. However, he had refused to predict his own grandson's future, with the belief that knowing the events beforehand would deprive Sarvadaman of the joys and sorrows of living a real life.

Sarvadaman brought his thoughts to the present and heard his grandfather say, 'Now this wasn't a common occurrence and took place only once in a thousand human years, that too for just a few moments. Brahma set about calculating the exact instant and Shiva, taking position on the North Pole, strung his longbow Pinak and nocked the dreaded Narayan Astra. The Devas watched with bated breath as the terrifying missile shot through the stars and found its mark, destroying the demons and their abodes in one massive explosion. Overjoyed, the Devas declared the day as a celebration of light and thus began the tradition of Dev-Deepawali that we celebrate even today.'

Sarvadaman was inspired by the larger-than-life imagery of the story and his determination to master the bow and arrow became even stronger. Eager for more, he asked his grandfather for another story, one related to Lord Vishnu, but the Brahmarishi answered cryptically, 'The tale that I just told you is from the past, but the one about the Bow of Vishnu that I want to share with you, is meant to happen in the future. I shall tell you about it when the time is right. For now concentrate on learning the correct use of this weapon.'

He took a couple of practice arrows lying nearby and showed them to the prince. 'Just as there are many factors that make a good bow, the same applies to arrows as well. Lighter arrows spend less time in the air, take a more direct route, and go further, while a heavier arrow, even though it cuts through the air better, has less speed and covers a shorter distance.'

He made his grandson feel the difference in the weight and texture of each arrow. 'An archer can even select multiple arrows with different dynamic spines that are deflected by varying amounts when they are released. This way, one can hit multiple targets by firing just once!'

Sarvadaman ran his fingers over the multi-coloured vanes made of different bird feathers. He picked up an arrow that had a crescent moon-shaped tip and asked, 'Why is the point of this arrow different, Pitamah? It looks more ornamental rather than functional.'

Vishwamitra gave him a sad smile and said, 'The more intricate the shape of an arrow, the deadlier is its impact. This beautiful looking arrow is specifically used to slice through the necks of the enemy.'

The prince seemed impressed with the realization that a small projectile could decapitate a grown man. Observing him, Vishwamitra said, 'The thought of maiming and killing any life form fills me with sadness, but Daman, you shall soon be donning the mantle of kingship and you must be prepared for any eventuality. I am a hermit, a sanyasi who has vowed never to take up arms but you, the future king of Hastinapur, may have to take them up for the protection of your people.'

The Chandravanshi crown prince understood the implications of the Brahmarishi's words and nodded in earnest. He had learnt and mastered the military arts well, but his real test, the absolute stamp of approval on his ability to become a respected ruler, would be on the battlefield.

Adhyaye 22

While Sarvadaman was training for his future role, his cousin Parshu-Raam had returned home. The Brahmin who had struck terror in the hearts of corrupt and evil rulers twenty-one times, had finally come back to his country. He had been received by Rishi Agastya on his arrival and taken to the purifying waters of the Saraswati, Ganga and finally the Brahmaputra to rid him of the burden of taking so many lives.

Vishwamitra knew that meeting his cousin would be a great learning experience for Sarvadaman, so he took permission from the boy's parents and the two set off for the grand closing ceremony of the twenty-one-year-long Ashwamedh Yagnya that had been awaiting Parshu-Raam's return. Taking the broad highways of central Nabhi-varsh, they made rapid progress on horseback towards the Sahyadri mountains, the venue of the event.

The foothills were thronging with thousands of people who had come to witness the homecoming of their hero. Sarvadaman was happy to see that his friend Rohitashwa and Brahmarishi Vasishth were present there too, along with Maharishi Kanav and many other sages whom he had never met before. He saw his uncle, King Deval, and was introduced to Parshu-Raam's

131

mother, Renuka, and his grandparents Maharishi Ruchik and Satyavati. As he stood on the sidelines, watching the elders prepare for the welcome of the much-lauded hero, the desire to be received in a similar fashion some day arose in his heart.

The entire hill echoed with the chants of 'Swasti' as the crowd parted to let their hero pass. Flowers and holy water were sprinkled on Parshu-Raam's head as he walked towards the Yagnya vedi with folded hands. He was tall, well-built and had deep hazel eyes that were curiously expressionless. His fair face was framed by a dense mane of hair and a thick beard that added to his leonine appearance.

The final Yagnya was conducted by Rishi Kashyap and Parshu-Raam. Sarvadaman was overwhelmed by the entire experience. Grand announcements were made and the Brahmins, Shudras and Vaishyas were declared the new Kshatriyas of this world that had been cleansed of corruption. Sarvadaman was impressed by the conviction with which his cousin laid down a new set of rules for righteous kingship. He was glad Vishwamitra had brought him for the ceremony.

He joined the other assembled guests in pouring the final oblations. After the ritual was over, Vishwamitra took Parshu-Raam aside and asked him to speak to the young prince. As he approached the man who was being referred to as an Avatar by the gathering, Sarvadaman could feel an intense positive energy radiating from him. Surprisingly, the man who had decimated an entire class of rulers was gentle and soft-spoken, and the prince was taken aback by his friendliness.

Raam put a hand on his shoulder and said, 'You, my cousin, shall be one of the few kings of the future hailing from the original Kshatriya lineage. The responsibility of following the directives laid down by me is greatest on you now!'

Sarvadaman nodded nervously and understood the implication: he could not let his cousin down otherwise it would set a bad example for other rulers. Parshu-Raam showed him the longbow of Lord Vishnu that he had used in his campaign. Sarvadaman caressed it gingerly, feeling a thrill run down his spine as the Sharang glowed with a blue effulgence. Since many other people were vying for Parshu-Raam's attention, the prince withdrew after touching his feet and taking his final blessings.

As Sarvadaman watched his cousin meet everyone with equal warmth and humility, he asked his grandfather how Parshu-Raam could maintain such equanimity and self-control.

Vishwamitra replied thoughtfully, 'Raam has become like the ocean that remains unchanged even though hundreds of rivers flow into it every day. Such a man performs his karma according to the will of god, without any desire for personal gain. That is the reason he is being compared to an avatar. Raam has surpassed even the most accomplished of yogis by showing the world how Karma-Yog can be followed without caring for the fruits of your actions. You, my boy, have a lot to learn from him.'

'I shall be honoured to follow his footsteps,' Sarvadaman said fervently. Then he added, 'Please also tell me about the divine weapons he possesses.'

The Brahmarishi knew the boy had taken a fancy to the longbow of Lord Vishnu and replied, hoping to make him understand that weapons like that were not easy to obtain. 'Raam received the celestial Bow of Lord Vishnu from his father who had received it from his own father. Their family is the keeper of this weapon because of their good karma. He also performed an arduous penance to please Lord Shiva and obtained His Axe, earning him the epithet Parshu-Raam.

'These divine arms cannot be yours unless the gods decide to bestow them on you in service of a higher purpose. But, let me tell you from my own experience that possessing even the most sophisticated weapons of the gods cannot ensure your victory. I learnt this the hard way and will be forever grateful to Brahmarishi Vasishth for opening my eyes to that truth. Rather than aspiring to these, you should seek to perfect your skill in the weapons you already possess.'

His grandson accepted the advice, but asked for something in return. 'Pitamah, if I give up the idea of attaining divine weapons, will you teach me a divine mantra that my enemies cannot counter?'

Vishwamitra realized with a smile that Sarvadaman would not be shaken off his ambition so easily. Putting his hand lovingly on the boy's head, he replied, 'All right then, I shall teach you the mantra for propitiating Varun, the lord of the oceans. The same mantra saved the life of Devrat in Harishchandra's court so you better pay attention.'

Before he began, Vishwamitra cautioned him, 'This is a very powerful verse, created by the amalgamation of Varun's beej mantra with the Gayatri mantra. By invoking this hymn, you shall be able to seek Lord Varun's help in surviving even the most insurmountable threat to your life.

'You are only the second person with whom I am sharing this mantra, so pay attention to the correct pronunciation and metre to get its desired effect. Now repeat after me—

aum jalbimbaye vidmahe,
neel purushaye dhimahi,
tanno varunaye prachodyat!'

Sarvadaman repeated the opening shloka thrice. Vishwamitra then taught him the next lines and asked him to practice them diligently while he wrapped up the proceedings and prepared for their departure. The prince didn't know it yet, but this verse would change his life one day.

Adhyaye 23

Back in Hastinapur, Sarvadaman was bursting with the
excitement of having met Parshu-Raam and the adulation
that he had seen him receive from even seasoned rishis. With
the aim of testing the power of the mantra given to him by
Vishwamitra, he headed to the banks of the Ganga, to a spot
that was not frequented by people. He did not want anyone's
help in what he was trying to do, otherwise the test wouldn't
be successful.

Tying his horse to a sal tree he climbed up to a sturdy
branch and dived into the gushing river. He had swum in it
a hundred times before and knew which parts of it were safe.
But today, he wanted to explore the treacherous portion that
he had always been careful to avoid in the past. There was
an eddy in the middle of the river and with powerful strokes,
he headed straight towards it. The otherwise placid waters of
the river were churning in a wide vortex around his intended
destination. The exercise made his heart beat faster; he almost
turned red with the effort that was required to stay afloat in
the strong current. As he neared the centre, he had to put
more and more power into each stroke. The force of the river
was far greater than he had imagined and the gushing waters

closed over him from all sides, plunging him face down into the whirlpool. After a moment of panic he tried to calm himself, reminding himself that he was here for a purpose.

He stopped fighting the current and allowed the waters to take him deeper into the Ganga. Concentrating on holding his breath, he kept his eyes open and took in the myriad varieties of aquatic life around him in the clear waters of the river. Finally, assessing himself to be sufficiently far below the surface, he chanted in his mind the verse that he had memorized.

At first nothing happened and he wondered if he had pronounced it correctly. He tried to recite it again but his lungs were bursting from the effort of holding his breath for so long and the air escaped through his lips in a gasp. Immediately water began rushing in through his mouth and nostrils. The pressure of the water above him and the complete loss of air were too much to overcome and he felt himself drowning. Panic engulfed his mind and he found himself floundering in the rapidly diminishing light, flailing his arms and legs helplessly. Just when his mind started shutting down and body began entering a state of stupor, two pairs of strong arms grabbed him firmly.

His mind registered a glimmer of hope but only fleetingly since he was being pulled downwards instead of towards the surface. He was either stark raving mad right now or he was being taken to the abode of Lord Varun, the resting place of all those who drowned. Vishwamitra had told him that Varun was the keeper of the cosmic order called 'Reet'. He was not merely the lord of water but also the equivalent of Yamraj for those who died in his domain. His last thoughts before he lost consciousness were of how the mantra had failed him.

Hours later, when he opened his eyes, he found himself lying on a circular bed in a dimly lit but luxuriously appointed room. He could breathe and move his limbs so he was clearly not dead. Out of the corner of his eye, he saw a door open and a girl enter. However, he was taken aback when he realized she had the upper body of a human and the tail of a fish! Sarvadaman rubbed his eyes in disbelief. He had heard of the Matsya or mer-people from his grandmother but he had never believed those stories to be true. When he looked again, the girl was walking towards him on two legs and he breathed a sigh of relief. As she came closer, he noticed her pale complexion and raven hair that spread around her head like a halo. Mesmerized by her surreal beauty, Sarvadaman couldn't stop himself from asking, 'Who are you, O divine beauty?'

The girl smiled, revealing a perfect set of teeth glittering like pearls. 'Puru Yuvraj,' she said in a melodious voice, 'you are in the abode of Maharaj Sarvasen, the king of all underwater creatures that thrive in the depths of Mother Ganga, from Kashi to Ganga-Hriday, where she meets the ocean. My people rescued you from the waters above because of the mantra that you chanted. They are on their way to the court of Maharaj Dushyant even as we speak, to inform him of your wellness. Meanwhile, I have been asked by my father to personally look after you.'

The mantra hadn't failed, Sarvadaman realized with delight. Rather, it had brought the creatures who owed their allegiance to Lord Varun to his aid.

He looked at the girl with renewed interest and asked, 'May I know your name? How do you and your people manage to survive under the river?'

'My name is Sunanda, though my father calls me Jahnavi in the honour of this great river. I have never had a problem breathing inside or out of the waters of Mother Ganga. From what I know, we, the mer-people, have lived in its depths for many generations now.'

'Fascinating,' Sarvadaman said, 'I never knew there was a kingdom extending through the length of the river and I doubt if my father also knows about it!' Sarvadaman was awestruck by the knowledge that someone could live so comfortably underwater. The room he was in was probably part of an elaborate dwelling that belonged to Maharaj Sarvasen.

'He does,' the princess replied with a smile. 'In fact all the kings along the banks of Mother Ganga know of our existence though some prefer to feign ignorance. We do not come to the surface unless it is a matter of urgency and no human can reach our kingdom. Unless, of course, he is hell-bent on drowning himself!'

Sarvadaman grinned sheepishly. 'I am sorry I put you in this position. I was testing the mantra that my grandfather, Brahmarishi Vishwamitra, taught me and foolishly ventured into the whirlpool. If it wasn't for the power of the mantra and the goodness of your family, I would have paid a very heavy price for my recklessness.'

Jahnavi nodded and asked him to partake of some refreshments. The young human was the first of his kind that she had had the chance to observe from such close quarters and she was more than happy to show him around. When Sarvadaman stepped out of the room with her, he was surprised to see the water receding whenever they took a step forward. It was as if they were enclosed in a bubble of air that allowed them to float in the water without letting it pass through.

The mer-people had built a city that defied all the laws of the physical world. It was lit by fire torches which did not get extinguished. When he expressed his amazement at this, Jahnavi told him about the use of a natural gas that was released in a controlled fashion from the gaps in the walls. It was magic of a kind he couldn't even fathom and he wondered if it was some advanced science that humans were not yet privy to. Perhaps in times to come humans on land could benefit from the advances of those living underwater, but for now he let himself enjoy the sights and muffled sounds of the mysterious city.

Who knew whether he would get the chance to visit this magical place again!

Adhyaye 24

The young prince of Hastinapur returned home from his sojourn loaded with precious jewels and treasures that dazzled the entire court. Dushyant and Shakuntala were livid at him for having tried something so dangerous but Menaka, who was visiting, intervened to save her grandson from their wrath. She reminded Shakuntala of the story she had told her about Indra's charioteer and how she had been enamoured by the prospect of exploring the underwater realms. Perhaps in some subconscious way, Sarvadaman, who had been a mere babe then, had imbibed that fascination as well.

On his part, the scion of Puruvansh was more than apologetic to his parents and his gurus and promised never to repeat such foolishness. To prove his sincerity, he plunged headfirst into a gruelling schedule of learning scriptures, practicing martial arts, attending mock courts and learning the arts that his grandmother, Menaka, was teaching him on her visits to the kingdom. His playmates, the lion cubs he had brought from the ashram, had also grown into adults and he wrestled with them often to develop his own strength.

After months of hard work began bearing fruit, Vishwamitra beamed with pleasure as he gave Sarvadaman his final lesson. 'You have learnt everything there is about kingship, governance, arts and the scriptures. It is a responsibility, not a privilege, to lead people towards the path of Dharma. But before you go out in the world, you need to be aware of the other kingdoms that are a part of our great nation. You know of Mahodayapur and Kosal, with whom we have family ties, but now it's time to fill in the details of the other dominions.'

The Brahmarishi took a stick and began plotting a rough map on the soft sand in front of them. 'Our country lies north of the ocean, and south of the snowy mountains of Himvaan. Besides the Great White mountains, seven other ranges or Kul-parvats criss-cross our length and breadth. The Shuktimat range cuts diagonally across the northwest while the Mahendra hills rise along the eastern coast. By the way, that is where Parshu-Raam is currently residing,' he said. 'If you ever need his help you know where to go.

'On the western coast, the upper reaches are formed by the Sahyadri while the lower ranges belong to the Malay group. The central region is dominated by the Riksha mountains, and right below them the Vindhyas stretch eastwards while the Paripatra travel westward.

'From these colossal mountains flow our mighty rivers—the Saraswati, Sindhu, Shatadru, Ganga, Yamuna, Chandrabhaga, Brahmaputra, and many others begin in the foothills of the Himvaan while the Rishikulya, Trisama and others originate from the Shuktimat and Mahendra mountains.'

'The rivers Vedasmriti, Chambal, Shipra and a few others flow from the Paripatra mountains; the Narmada and Surasa from the Vindhyas; Tapti, Payoshni and Nirvindhya from the Riksha mountains; the Godavari, Bhimarathi, Krishna and others from the Sahyadri; and the Kritamala, Tamraparni and others from the Malaya hills.'

'What about the people living inside the rivers?' Sarvadaman asked excitedly.

'There aren't too many of those, my child,' Vishwamitra replied. 'King Sarvasen and his kind are found only in the Saraswati and Ganga, though there are other mer-people living deep in the ocean. Only a very small population of underwater beings thrives well in fresh waters.'

An image, long suppressed, now flashed in Sarvadaman's mind—Princess Jahnavi with a fish tail. The Brahmarishi sensed the question plaguing his pupil and said, 'Yes, the mer-people have the ability to appear as humans in situations where their piscine appendages are useless. They have great gifts to offer humans, but can also be equally vicious in protecting their own territory. It's only because of the Varun mantra that they came to your aid the other day so you better not tempt fate like that again.'

Sarvadaman apologized once again, 'I know I was reckless, Pitamah, but you have to agree that if it hadn't been for that misadventure, I would never have found out about these people!'

'And you would not have met Jahnavi,' Vishwamitra retorted with a twinkle in his eyes.

Sarvadaman turned red with embarrassment; he couldn't discuss such matters with his grandfather! But the Brahmarishi looked at him kindly and said, 'You can never control the invisible strings that draw you towards a kindred soul. But you must get to know her well before you make up your mind about any kind of future with her.'

The prince nodded meekly, still embarrassed about having the conversation, so Vishwamitra said, 'Coming back to our lesson, do you know why our country is known as Nabhi-varsh?'

'Yes, Gurudev, I remember you telling me before that the appellation is in honour of Maharaj Nabhi, the great-grandson of Manu, the first man. He was the son of Maharaj Agnidhra, who ruled over the entire Jambu-dweep, and his wife, the Apsara Purvachitti.'

'Very good,' Vishwamitra said appreciatively. 'Just remember that all this happened in the very first Manvantar while now we are in the seventh.'

Sarvadaman scratched his head and said, 'Can you please tell me the divisions of time once again? I am sorry my mind just doesn't absorb these mathematical calculations.'

Vishwamitra said with resignation, 'I am explaining these for the very last time; you better pay attention. Srishti-Karta Brahma has a life span of one hundred years. Each of these years is made up of three hundred and sixty days, known as kalpas, and as many nights. Just as each of our days is divided into four prehars comprising twelve hours, Brahma's kalpas are divided into fourteen Manvantars. We are presently nearing the afternoon of the first kalpa of Brahma's fifty-first year. Maharaj Nabhi began ruling this country in the first Manvantar of this kalpa and now we are in the seventh Manvantar. Just as each hour of our day is further divided into seconds, the Manvantars are divided into seventy-one Mahayugs.'

Sarvadaman's head was reeling once again with the numbers but he noted down the explanation, vowing to read it on his own later and Vishwamitra decided to not digress too much from the topic at hand. As the Brahmarishi resumed the lesson, he began marking the kingdoms of Nabhi-varsh on the makeshift map. 'Starting from the Sindhu river in the north, the kingdoms that stretch along our northern and eastern borders are Gandhar, Kashyap-mir, Kaikeya, Madra, Trigarta, Puru, Mahodayapur, Kosal, Videha, Magadh, Anga, Pundra, Kamarupa, Sonit and Lauhitya.

'Along the eastern coast and moving southwards are Vanga, Utkala, Kaling, Taling, Andhra and Dravid. When we trace our journey back from the southern tip, upwards along the western coast, we have Mushik, Kishkindha, Gomanta, Konkan, Ashmak, Saurashtra, Anarta, Abhira, Sauvira and finally the kingdom of Sindhu, bringing us right back to where we started.

'In the middle are the kingdoms of Matsya, Nishad, Shursen, Kashi, Chedi, Vatsa and Avanti. The last was ruled by Kartavirya Arjun, who reigned over the globe quite well before Ravan corrupted him and set him on the path to his demise at the hands of Parshu-Raam. The Asur Lord of Lanka is currently in hiding, trying to propitiate Lord Shiva, but he will return soon enough.'

Pointing to the regions outside the boundary of the nation, he said, 'East of Nabhi-varsh dwell the Kiraats while on the west are the Yavans. In the north are the Hara-Huns and Shakyas and in the south, on the island of Lanka, are the Asurs. As you can see, we are surrounded by Mlecchas, people who have been losing the path of Dharma steadily. The Tretayug is at its peak and such deviations are expected but you have to be aware of them.'

Concluding the lesson, he said, 'Raam has carefully selected the kings who adhere to Dharma, but things may

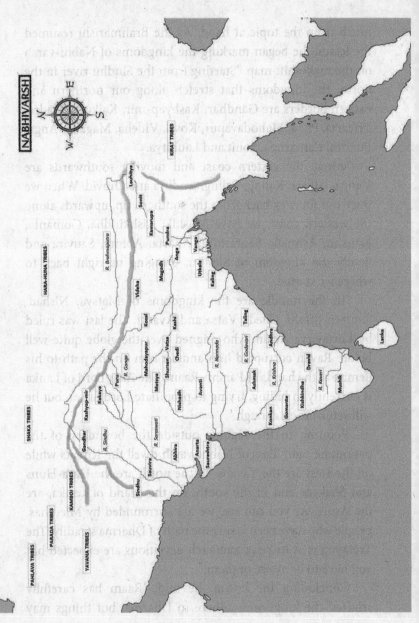

change once the memory of his carnage has dimmed. If there is one thing that I have learnt in my lifetime, it is that the more the things change, the more they tend to remain the same. Nabhi-varsh is the best division of Jambu-dweep, where people still follow the doctrine of karma. We are lucky to have been born in this hallowed land and you are luckier that you will get the opportunity to shape the Puru kingdom into a beacon of civilization for the other kingdoms. It will give me great pleasure to inform your father that the time to pass the onus of kingship has arrived.'

Sarvadaman folded his hands in gratitude to the guru who had taught him not just the intricacies of Dharma and politics but also the path he had to take in the future. Vishwamitra blessed him wholeheartedly. When the tenuous peace that had been established by Parshu-Raam came to an end, someone would have to assume the responsibility of restoring order. He hoped Sarvadaman would be able to rise to the challenge.

Adhyaye 25

Sunlight streamed in through the latticework into the royal chamber. Clad in deep blue robes, Dushyant sat on a luxurious futon next to the windows. The years had added a certain nobility to his features and the hair greying at his temples gave him an even more imperial air than before. Shakuntala, who had aged as gracefully as her husband, sat beside him, looking resplendent in a sea-green sari. Her skin was still as pure and flawless as the first time she had met Dushyant and although she wouldn't admit it openly, she was secretly grateful to her Apsara genes for that. Facing the two, sat Acharya Dirghatamas and Brahmarishi Vishwamitra, their ochre clothes a stark contrast to the royal couples' regal finery.

Sarvadaman stood nearby, bursting with excitement. The thought of becoming the next ruler of Hastinapur spun and danced in his mind and he was desperately waiting for his father's approval now. He was almost twenty, about the same age Dushyant had been when he had been crowned king. His body was shaped to perfection and confidence oozed from every pore.

Acharya Dirghatamas, being the most senior member of the council as well as the kulguru, began the discussion, saying

'Maharaj, it is no secret that your rule has brought about a new era of prosperity to the Puru kingdom. With the help of your brothers, you have redrawn the boundaries of our land and extended them to Kashyap-mir and Gandhar. You have ruled your subjects with the compassion of a father and the strength of a true leader.'

Dushyant acknowledged the glowing tribute with characteristic humility and folded hands. The kulguru, who was well advanced in age now, bowed his head too and continued, 'Our shastras urge each human being to pursue the four goals of dharma, artha, kama and moksh and to enable that, our ancient rishis devised the logical stages of Brahmacharya, Grihasth, Vanprasth and, finally, Sanyas. The Varna-ashram dharma is the guiding principle of all Arya nations and according to these sacred laws, the time has come for you to relinquish the throne.'

'Gurudev, I fully intend to uphold the requirements of Dharma so that the next generation can fulfil its responsibilities. With the blessings of Brahmarishi Vishwamitra, Sarvadaman is ready to take the reins of the kingdom and I am more than willing to hand them over to him, just as my father had intended to pass them to me.'

As Vishwamitra nodded his agreement, Sarvadaman bowed to his elders and said, 'If you believe I am ready to sit on the moon throne, Father, it is only by the grace of my gurus, Acharya Dirghatamas and Pitamah. I understand that kingship is not a right but a responsibility, and I shall be honoured to follow in your footsteps and try to emulate your achievements.' He bent and touched the feet of all the elders.

Shakuntala's eyes filled with tears as she blessed her son. 'From the moment I learnt of your existence I have dreamt of seeing you on the moon throne. Although the circumstances of your ascension are quite different from what I had imagined then, and infinitely better, I am glad to see you finally attain your rightful position in the world!'

Just then a sudden gust of fragrant wind entered the chamber and Menaka appeared out of thin air. Sarvadaman rushed to his grandmother to take her blessings and she embraced him, kissing the top of his head. It always amazed him how devastatingly gorgeous his grandmother was even though she was older than all the people present in that room. For a fleeting moment the image of Jahnavi flashed in front of his eyes and he made himself a mental promise to see her again, soon.

When the celestial visitor had settled down, she revealed the purpose behind her visit. 'The Tretayug has reached its zenith and the preparations for its passing shall shortly begin. Before Dvaparyug sets in, the Devas wish to see Nabhi-varsh in such a position that it can help the other nations of Jambu-dweep tide through the difficult times ahead.'

Vishwamitra was the first to respond. 'I see you are still carrying on the good work of our mutual friend,' he said, making a sly reference to Indra.

Menaka knew better than to take the bait. They had finally become friends after years of hostility and she was not willing to let it all go because of a careless remark. She gave the Brahmarishi her sweetest smile and replied, 'Yes, my lord, we Apsaras have no option but to stay loyal to the lord of Swarg. And as you pointed out, he *is* a friend so I thought it prudent to bring the news to my family myself rather than send it through a messenger.'

The Brahmarishi bowed his head in acknowledgement, ceding this round to the Apsara.

Menaka now addressed the others. 'The Devas had high hopes from the global empire established by Kartavirya Arjun but his corruption by the Asurs left them disappointed. Thankfully the menace was effectively countered by the selfless and brave actions of Parshu-Raam.'

Deftly catching on to her train of thought, Vishwamitra said, 'And since both these men were born in Nabhi-varsh, Shakra wants someone from this country to take up the responsibility of advancing human civilization. Isn't it a bit unfair to put so much pressure on one nation?'

Menaka nodded in agreement and said, 'For once I fully concur! I have witnessed the hardships Raam faced and I would not wish those on anyone. However, as things stand, the only country that is poised to become the beacon of spiritual enlightenment right now is Nabhi-varsh. This is an indication that even the gods are supporting your efforts so I would say we should make the most of it.'

Sarvadaman quietly chuckled at his grandmother's irreverent tone and saw Vishwamitra smile.

'This could well be the opportunity Puruvansh has been waiting for,' Dirghatamas said. 'I am sure there are many worthy kings in the reckoning but I am confident that Yuvraj Sarvadaman shall emerge as the most appropriate choice among them all.'

Dushyant and Shakuntala smiled. With the support of the Devas, their son could well become the most illustrious ruler of the lunar dynasty. Vishwamitra interrupted their thoughts and said, 'Since we are all in agreement, let us initiate the process of transfer of power as soon as possible. I recommend that the coronation be held on the day of Holi on Falgun Purnima. Let the festival celebrating the arrival of spring also usher in a new reign for the Puru kingdom.'

Everyone agreed to the proposal and the family burst into congratulatory celebrations. Dushyant embraced his son with tears of pride. The circle of life was endless—it was when his own coronation was announced that he had found Shakuntala and now their son had come of age to take over the responsibility of the kingdom.

Dushyant's brothers and their families were summoned and the happy news shared with them before a formal announcement was made to the court. The women left for further discussion on the ceremonies while the men began making lists of the guests who would have to be invited. The palace staff was informed of the grand preparations for the ceremony and sweets were ordered for distribution to the citizens of the kingdom. Professional announcers were sent to the farthest corners of the kingdom to allow those who wished to attend the ceremony enough time for the preparations. Missives were to be sent to all neighbouring kingdoms and adequate arrangements for the lodging and housing of all the guests who would be attending were discussed.

Sarvadaman slipped out of the melee after a lot of congratulatory backslaps and friendly chatter. There was one particular guest that he wanted to invite by himself—the princess of the underwater kingdom of the Ganga.

Adhyaye 26

As he made his way to the river, Sarvadaman thought of how his urge to see Princess Jahnavi again became stronger after each meeting. It was almost as if her company reinforced his desire to spend more time with her in a never-ending loop. He didn't need to drown any more to meet her; his mere presence in the water was enough to alert her to his arrival. They had been meeting at the same spot in secret for several months. Now that he was about to be crowned, he wanted to find out if she felt the same way about him as he did for her and if she was willing to act on it. The soft sand on the banks of the majestic Ganga was pristine white. He dived into the cool waters of the river for a short swim while he waited.

Within moments, Jahnavi was by his side, watching him frolic with the Gangetic dolphins. He was holding on to the fin of one of the benign creatures, grinning as they leapt in and out of the river, dragging him along. She laughed, watching his antics; he always managed to bring a smile to her face.

Jahnavi found Daman, as she called him, really good company. Unlike the other princes she had seen, he was without any trace of arrogance, and whenever they were together he made her laugh so much that she forgot the worries of her kingdom. Sarvasen's tribe was shrinking; within a few generations their numbers had dwindled from thousands to hundreds and this bothered him. There had been talk of moving to the ocean to be closer to other mer-people but Jahnavi didn't wish to leave the river that had given her her name as well as her whole life.

The moment Sarvadaman noticed her presence he released his hold on the dolphin and swam towards her. Jahnavi was in a playful mood and began swimming away from him. She looked at him with a naughty smile and zipped past him into the deep water of the river.

'Damn,' Sarvadaman thought, 'she is using her fish tail again to outswim me.'

He had mastered the art of underwater breathing over the past few months, and caught up with her soon enough. After a short game of hide-and-seek he saw her moving towards the surface of the river and followed her. They climbed out of the water at almost the same time and flopped on the soft sand, laughing. Sarvadaman's heart seemed to be galloping away on its own chariot as he saw her lying beside him.

Jahnavi's waist-length raven hair spread out behind her head, and her wet angavastra clung to her body, accentuating her soft curves. Her pale complexion, courtesy of a lifetime spent underwater, always turned a little red in the glare from the sun. Her eyes were dark like the deep waters of the river and when he gazed into them, he felt a strange anxiety in his stomach, as if something earth-shattering would happen if he were to look away.

He knew his fears were irrational but he couldn't help feeling that way. Calming himself, he told her about his impending coronation.

'That is wonderful news, Daman, I am so happy for you!' Jahnavi was ecstatic. 'So, now I will have to address you as *Maharaj*?'

Sarvadaman laughed self-consciously and shook his head. 'No,' he said, 'for you I shall always remain Daman.' He took her hand in his and, looking into her eyes, said nervously, 'We have known each other for a while now and I hope what I'm about to say won't offend you in any way.'

Jahnavi looked at the sombre expression on his face and snatched her hand away, laughing. 'Nothing you say can offend me, my friend! Tell me what's bothering you?'

The prince swallowed hard and said, 'We both enjoy each other's company. I know I really do . . . I hope you feel the same?' he looked at her for confirmation. Jahnavi nodded, unsure of where he was headed.

Emboldened he forged into the unchartered territory of human emotions and said, 'My father will start looking for a suitable bride for me after the coronation. I am a fairly simple man, and I wish to be with someone who is like-minded. I do not want a wife who will merely accompany me to ceremonial gatherings but a woman who has an independent mind and can take care of herself, with whom I can share my ideas and dreams.'

'Well, that is quite understandable,' Jahnavi said, 'but why are you telling me all this?'

'Because,' Sarvadaman said earnestly, 'I want that woman to be you!'

Jahnavi's own heart began beating faster at that and she exclaimed incredulously, 'What? Are you playing with me, Daman? If you are, trust me I'll personally drown you in the river this time!'

But Sarvadaman did not smile. His face was contorted into a grimace as if he was experiencing great physical pain. He steadied his mind and said, 'I am not jesting with you Jahnavi. Whenever I am with you, I feel like a better person. I don't know if you feel the same for me but if you do, can we give this relationship a try?'

Jahnavi saw that he was serious. She took a few moments to compose her own thoughts before answering. 'Ever since you've entered my life my perspective on things has changed as well. I have begun exploring life outside our submarine kingdom and have discovered numerous new joys that life has to offer. But, I have always thought of us as friends; marrying outside our community is strictly forbidden for mer-people.'

'But don't you see! That is precisely the reason the numbers of your tribe have been steadily declining! If you were free to marry any other being like us humans, your clan would have thrived and perhaps displaced these dolphins in the entire river by now.'

Jahnavi gave him a light slap on the wrist and said with mock anger, 'Don't you dare say anything about my clan! Even if it happens to be the correct analysis of the situation.' Looking at him with a fierce expression, she added, 'It is not as simple as that for us, Daman. You humans can live in any environment, from deserts to the snowy mountains, but we can only thrive in the fresh waters of the Ganga and Saraswati. Even the salt waters of the ocean are not really conducive for our constitution. My father has been toying with the idea of doing just that but the thought of marrying me off to a human will be overwhelming!'

Sarvadaman nodded in understanding, but asked, 'Leave that aside, what about your own feelings? Do you think you can find it in your heart to love me as a husband and not just a friend?'

Jahnavi knew she had to answer the question truthfully; not just for his sake but for her own as well. This time she took his hand in hers. 'I cannot guarantee how my heart will feel for you in the future, but I know for sure that we shall add joy and adventure to each other's lives. I don't know if that is enough to sustain a marriage but I can promise to be with you as your friend all your life.'

Sarvadaman's face finally relaxed and he said, 'The best marriages are between people who live as friends. I do not see myself falling head over heels in love with anyone, but I do love my friends with a passion. I did not expect an immediate response from you; I just wanted you to ponder over the idea.' Jahnavi nodded quietly. He added, 'Do let me know if you think my proposal is acceptable otherwise we shall continue to remain the good friends that we are.'

Adhyaye 27

Voices filled the Royal Hall of Hastinapur, bouncing off the two dozen marble pillars that supported the high vaulted ceiling. Dushyant, the king of Puru, sat on the chariot-like moon throne for the very last time. His heart was filled with a happiness that he couldn't have imagined. He realized how happy his father Aileen must have been when he had decided to make Dushyant the king, and now that the time had come, he couldn't wait to crown his own son.

Bathed in the warm sunlight that enveloped the palace, nay the entire city, with its radiance, Dushyant found himself becoming philosophical. Life was just like the transition of seasons, he thought. Spring was the time of fresh hopes and so was his son's coronation. With the change of season, nature had quite literally burst into a thousand possibilities. Hastinapur had come alive with the sounds of birds getting out of their winter slumber and showing off their colourful plumage. The road leading to the palace was festooned and lined with small pedestals holding vessels full of powdered tesu flowers that would be used later for the festivities. The entire palace was decked up like a bride and the royal family, with their glittering jewels and silken finery, were fanned out around the moon throne. Acharya Dirghatamas, Maharishi Kanav, Brahmarishi Vishwamitra and Parshu-Raam stood beside the throne while Sarvadaman sat in the place of the charioteer, right in front of and below Dushyant's seat.

Visiting dignitaries were seated in the hall along with the councillors, and among them were Jahnavi and Maharaj Sarvasen. The royal family of Kanyakubja was also present and the young sons of King Deval bowed when Sarvadaman caught their eye, giving him confidence in the position he was about to step into.

At the auspicious hour for the Abhishekam, the kulguru blew into a conch to signal the beginning of the proceedings and a hush fell on the hundreds who had gathered to witness the event. The four senior rishis took possession of gold vessels that had been filled with waters from the Sindhu in the west, Ganga in the north, Brahmaputra in the east and Kaveri in the south. Dipping mango leaves into the sanctified waters they sprinkled it on the throne and its occupants while chanting sacred verses.

Another vessel, filled with the waters of the Saraswati, was handed over to Dushyant who was now joined by Shakuntala. Together they poured the water on the head of their son who sat facing the crowd with his hands folded in salutation. It was an important occasion for Sarvadaman and he was savouring every moment.

As the chants continued and were picked up by other learned Brahmins, the entire hall began to resonate with the sacred sounds of Vedic hymns. The prince was anointed with sandalwood, turmeric and vermilion and showered with the petals of marigold and champa flowers. A new robe made of blue tussar silk, embroidered with green emeralds and silver thread, was draped on his shoulders. Finally Dushyant placed the glittering Puru crown on his son's head.

His words rang through the assembled crowd as he declared, 'By the power vested in me by the laws of the first man, Manu, I hereby declare Sarvadaman the new king of Hastinapur. I wish you a reign that is longer than any of your predecessors and more successful than anyone in the Chandravansh!'

Sarvadaman bowed to his elders as the gathering burst into spontaneous applause. There was a shower of flowers and blessings in the general direction of the throne and the royal family beamed with pride. Dushyant and Shakuntala led Sarvadaman to the throne that they had occupied before. Once he had taken his seat, the kulguru took the royal sword from Dushyant and passed it to its new owner amidst renewed shouts of 'Swasti' from the gathering.

Acharya Dirghatamas blessed the new king with a successful tenure and made another announcement: 'Citizens of Hastinapur, I have discharged the duty of chief-preceptor to three generations of the Puru family. Today, as our new king begins his reign, the time has come for me to retire. I hereby abdicate from the post of kulguru and offer it to Brahmarishi Vishwamitra.'

Dirghatamas had discussed his decision with Dushyant earlier but the rest of the congregation was surprised. Sarvadaman's face beamed with happiness as he realized that his grandfather and guru would be his guide in the future as well. Brahmarishi Vishwamitra folded his hands and bowed to Acharya Dirghatamas in acceptance of his offer. 'This is not the first time that I have been asked to step into the shoes of a learned guru; it seems I work best when asked to substitute for someone else!' he said with a self-deprecating smile.

There was polite laughter from the crowd and he proceeded in a more serious tone, 'Not long ago I had taken over the responsibility of being kulguru to the Suryavansh, but I knew at the very onset that it was going to be a temporary position. Acharya Dirghatamas does me great honour by offering me the responsibility for the Puru kingdom. I assure him that I shall try to justify his faith in me with utmost sincerity.'

There was another round of applause to welcome the well-known, and somewhat notorious, Brahmarishi officially into the Puru fold and Vishwamitra bowed to the audience. Then he signalled to the attendants to let the ceremony continue. The councillors came forward with gifts for the new king. They were followed by rulers and representatives of neighbouring kingdoms who brought exquisite offerings of rare birds and animals, baskets of exotic fruits, weapons of unalloyed strength, gold, silver and precious stones. Jahnavi gifted him a necklace of tear-drop shaped pearls with a look of happiness and pride that did not escape Shakuntala's notice. She looked at Sarvadaman's face and saw the same happiness reflected on it. It didn't take her long to realize that her son had truly grown up, and tender feelings of love had begun blooming in his heart. She looked at the retreating form of the princess of the underwater domains and let out a sigh of contentment. There would be difficulties ahead for them but she promised herself that she would be supportive of any decision Sarvadaman took for his happiness.

When the last visitor had made his offering and then resumed his seat, Vishwamitra stood up once again and said, 'The festival of colours signifies the victory of Lord Narasimha over the dreaded demon Hiranyakashyapu. On this day, Shri Hari Vishnu rid the three worlds of the tyranny of the Daitya who had gained a boon of conditional immortality from Srishti-Karta Brahma. With the death of the evil Asur Swarg was restored to the Devas, and on earth a new breed of Dharmik rulers, like his son Prahlad, took over. Today, we celebrate the crowning of another ruler who we hope will be as just and courageous as Bhakt Prahlad.

'For those who are prisoners of the calendar,' he said to conclude the proceedings, 'spring comes but once a year. But for those of us, who have the good fortune of having our friends and family by our side, every day marks the arrival of spring. King Sarvadaman is valued not only by his family but also his people, and with his parents' permission, I would like to give him the title of "Bharat", the cherished one.'

He looked at the faces of the royal family and saw approval in their eyes. Dushyant and Shakuntala gave their consent and the hall rang with chants of 'Long live Maharaj Bharat!' The Brahmarishi blew into his conch and declared, 'It is believed that when Narasimha defeated the demon, the denizens of the higher lokas were so delighted by the removal of the cloud of darkness that they showered each other with the colours of the rainbow. Following the same tradition, I request our new king, Raja Bharat, to declare the festival open and let the citizens smear each other with the colours of spring.'

Bharat savoured the sound of his new name, rolling it off his tongue. He stood up from the throne and bowed to his parents, family and assembled dignitaries. Then in a loud voice, he proclaimed, 'Let the festivities begin!'

Fistfuls of colour began flying in the air as the crowd broke into lusty shouts of 'Holi hai!' The royal family and guests politely applied small quantities of vermilion on each other but Sarvadaman walked boldly towards Jahnavi and smeared her forehead with the auspicious colour of spring and fertility. As he touched her cheek, he was glad to see that the blush on her face was not just a result of the gulaal he had applied.

Adhyaye 28

Dushyant and Shakuntala watched the transition of their son from a prince to a king with pride. However, there was still one aspect of his life—his marriage—that they wished to take care of before they took Vanprasth and retired to the forest.

The royal family used to dine together in the royal dining hall, but tonight, Dushyant had asked Bharat to come to his own chamber. Bharat was glad to get an opportunity to spend some quality time with his parents. The moment he entered the room, a delectable aroma wafted into his nostrils. Like any child, the taste of the food cooked by his mother held a special place in his heart. The fragrance and the simplicity of her cooking reminded him of his childhood and his mouth began to water in anticipation of the delicious food that awaited him.

When Shakuntala saw his expression, her face broke into a broad smile. Without wasting any time she asked the maids to bring water in a vessel to wash the king's hands and feet. Finishing the ablutions, Bharat sat down cross-legged on the cushions that had been placed on the floor. Dushyant and Shakuntala also sat down beside him while the attendants placed three short stools and plates in front of them and began serving the food.

There was roasted and mashed eggplant that was flavoured
with bits of ginger, cumin and wisps of coriander; the lentils
had been simmered slowly on a wood fire with hints of
nutmeg and cinnamon; the simple long-grain steamed rice
gave off an enticing aroma of saffron and cardamom and
there was a thick gravy dish made of chickpeas garnished with
fenugreek, pomegranate seeds and dried mango powder. To
add to this there was crisp flatbread, perfectly done in a clay
oven, served with dollops of home-made butter, and to wash
it all down was a collection of the finest wines available in
Nabhi-varsh.

Bharat's eyes widened seeing all his favourite dishes
together. 'Wow!' he said, pleasantly surprised. 'Mother, you
have prepared everything that I love!'

He took a deep breath, savouring the aromas, but didn't
touch the food. Shakuntala looked at him quizzically and
he smiled and said, 'This food, which you have prepared so
lovingly, would taste even better if you fed it to me with your
own hands.'

Shakuntala was more than happy to oblige her beloved
son. She broke a morsel of bread, dipped it in the chickpea
gravy and offered it to him. 'Feeding you with my own hands
after so long is a pleasure,' she said. 'Sometimes I feel the days
spent in the forest, even though less luxurious, were simpler
and more joyful.'

Bharat nodded but Dushyant countered her statement
good-naturedly, 'I don't agree since you did not have my
company in the forest!'

Shakuntala laughed and said playfully, 'Yes, we didn't
and that's why life was simpler; now I can't even lift a finger
without ten maids running to my rescue! And to add to the

complication, I do not even know what to call my son any more. Is it Sarvadaman or Bharat?'

'It is all for your comfort, my dear,' Dushyant said, smiling. 'You can't blame me for taking care of my family. And as for the name, he'll always be our little subduer-of-all in the privacy of our chambers. But for the outside world, he is Raja Bharat now.'

Bharat smiled seeing the loving banter between his parents. He knew there had been misunderstandings and bitterness in the past, but, from the moment they had arrived in Hastinapur, Dushyant had spoilt them both with his attention. Thinking about it now, Bharat was glad they had not ended up like some other dysfunctional families where people's egos ruled their relationships.

As the conversation turned to what was happening in the kingdom, the king told Dushyant, 'I am spending a lot of time towards strengthening the army and evaluating the resources we have currently. To begin with, there aren't enough fighting men thanks to my cousin Parshu-Raam. However, now that anyone from any class of society can take up arms and become a Kshatriya, we should be able to remedy the situation.'

Dushyant nodded as Shakuntala fed her son small morsels of food. The new king of Hastinapur shared more details. 'My first step was to conduct drafting exercises to increase the strength of the army to that of one full Akshauhini,' he said, explaining his plans for the basic division of any Arya army that comprised the infantry, cavalry, chariot-riders and elephants. 'That will give us enough soldiers to face attacks from multiple directions. Our generals are touring the kingdom in search of young aspirants of both sexes and so far, the reports have been encouraging. I hope your fiery generals will continue to inspire future generations of fighters.

'Actually, the bigger concern right now is securing enough food for such an enormous army! Maintaining the sheer number of men, women, horses and elephants will require massive resources so I have asked our scientists and agriculturists to find ways to boost food production as well as create new varieties of crops that can give higher yields.'

Seeing Dushyant's smile of approval, he continued, 'The other, even more pressing problem is manufacturing enough arms and ammunition, armour and equipment for the various divisions, archers, mace fighters, spear fighters, swordsmen, infantry, cavalry as well their mounts. We'll need huge quantities of iron for this. Pitamah has very graciously mediated a treaty with the ore-rich forest kingdoms of the Nishads in central Nabhi-varsh. He has also put in motion an effective system of spies to gather data about the activities in the neighbouring kingdoms and enlisted Maharaj Sarvasen's sons to help train a troop of underwater warriors.'

Dushyant and Shakuntala exchanged a look at the mention of the mer-king and realized that the Brahmarishi had his own ways of utilizing the opportunities time presented.

The three spent the next hour enjoying the delicious food and each other's company. Once the meal was over the king fell back on the cushion with his eyes closed. 'Ma, your cooking is absolutely divine,' he said with a sigh of contentment.

Shakuntala smiled and replied, 'Have as much of it as you can now. After you get married, you won't have time to eat the food cooked by your mother.'

Bharat shook his head and said, 'No woman on earth is worth leaving this heavenly food for!'

Dushyant took a cue from his wife and asked his son in a nonchalant tone, 'Talking of girls, is there anyone special that you want to tell us about?'

Bharat sat up with a start and asked suspiciously, 'Why would you ask that?'

'No particular reason,' Shakuntala said innocently. 'It's just that ever since your coronation we have been receiving proposals from kingdoms far and wide for your hand. We thought it better to ask if you have already found someone suitable, instead of forcing our choice on you.'

Bharat grinned. 'So this was all a trick? Plying me with my favourite dishes was a ploy to make me open up.'

His mother came back with a quick retort. 'That depends on whether or not you have something to open up about!'

The king smiled. 'As a matter of fact, I do have someone I have been meaning to talk to you both about—it is Jahnavi, the daughter of Maharaj Sarvasen. I have been spending a lot of time with her and I feel she would be the perfect companion for me and an excellent queen for Hastinapur.'

'I knew it!' Shakuntala said triumphantly. 'A mother's eyes can never be deceived. I saw the way the two of you were gazing at each other on the day of the coronation and figured out what was going on.'

Bharat had no idea his mother had been so perceptive and blushed at the reference.

Laughing, Dushyant patted his shoulder and said, 'She is a fine woman! Brahmarishi Vishwamitra has also mentioned the opportunity that an association with the royal family of the underwater realms can provide Hastinapur.'

Bharat nodded sheepishly. 'Yes, Pitamah did broach the subject with me casually.' He shook his head in disbelief—his love life hadn't even begun properly and everyone in his family was already aware of it.

'Your mother and I agree with your choice,' Dushyant said, 'not just because of the alliance that will be forged with this marriage, but also because we know you and the princess will complement each other. You are ambitious while she is stable; you are restless like a tornado while she is calm like the depths of the Ganga. Together you will help balance each other's personalities. But,' he said after a pause, 'you must remember one thing: Jahnavi is not a human. It is almost impossible for a human being to have a child with non-human races like the Gandharvs, Yakshas, Kinnars, Vanars and Asurs. So far the most successful pairings have been between humans and Nagas and humans and Apsaras.'

'What are you saying, Father?' Bharat asked perplexed.

Dushyant replied in a practical tone, 'You have our blessings for this alliance because we know she makes you happy. But you should keep in mind that she may never be able to bear you a child. The love of a woman may be enough for a man to live all his life without an issue, but a kingdom cannot do without an heir.'

Adhyaye 29

Barely a week later Bharat received news of skirmishes on the northwestern borders of the Puru kingdom. According to Brahmarishi Vishwamitra's spies, the assault was being perpetrated by an alliance of five tribes from the north and west—the Panch Gann.

An emergency meeting of the council was called to discuss what needed to be done. The commander-in-chief of the army, Senapati Vikramjeet, a tanned, well-built man of indeterminate age with a fierce moustache, addressed the gathering, 'We cannot take any hasty steps. The Five, as they are referring to themselves, are the Pahlavs, Kambojs, Shakas, Yavans and Paradas. Some of these people are our own distant relatives so we must carefully consider the situation before taking any step against them.'

'How are they related to us?' Bharat asked the senapati, who looked towards the kulguru for enlightenment.

'If his highness permits,' Vishwamitra replied formally, 'I shall take this opportunity to present a detailed map of Nabhi-varsh before we go into further discussion.'

Bharat nodded. Moments later a map showing the kingdoms of the northern mountains, eastern highlands, deccan plateau and southern deltas was brought and placed on the central table. The councillors gathered around for a look.

Taking a stick in his hand, Vishwamitra began pointing, 'The northwestern kingdoms of Pahlav, Kamboj, Gandhar, Sauvira and Sindhu have mostly been settled by the Anavs and Druhyus who are descendants of Maharaj Yayati's sons Anu and Druhyu.'

Bharat was trying to remember the basic family chart and said, 'If my memory serves me, Maharaj Yayati is considered the forefather of all Chandravanshi Arya nations. With his two wives, Devyani and Sharmishtha, he sired the clans that settled in different locations. While the central region between the Saraswati and Ganga was settled by us Purus, the Druhyus and Anavs moved westwards beyond the boundaries of Nabhi-varsh. The other two—Turvashas and Yadus—went southwards, and populated the western and peninsular parts of Nabhi-varsh.'

The Brahmarishi nodded approvingly and said, 'Your memory indeed serves you well, my king. Westwards of Gandhar are the lands of the Yavans and Vahliks, while above the mountains of Kashyap-mir are the principalities of the Shakas and Hara-Huns. All of them have fought amongst each other before, but had been lying low for a while. I had a feeling they would set their eyes on Nabhi-varsh soon.'

The senior council members murmured in agreement; Dushyant's reign had largely been peaceful because these mercenary tribes were busy fighting with each other.

The senapati took the stick from Vishwamitra and said, 'The attacks started as minor skirmishes along the border but the kulguru's spies have reported sightings of multiple groups of mounted soldiers coming from the direction of Nisa.' He pointed to the city marked on the map. 'This is the capital of the Pahlavs, located on a major trade route connecting the fledgling western nations to the older ones in the east. The kingdom itself produces an abundance of grains, grapes, silver and leather goods. Perhaps all the wealth they have amassed has gone to their head. For all intents and purposes, they seem to be leading this attack. Ironically, they are the worshippers of Mitra, the patron god of friendship!'

Bharat absorbed the information and his uncle Vasu, Dushyant's youngest brother who was the only person from the family remaining in the council, said, 'I agree with the senapati's assessment. While the Yavans, Paradas and Shakas are a restless lot they lack the resources to fund an all-out war against Nabhi-varsh. The Kambojs are by and large a peaceful people. It must be the Pahlav king Parvatak who convinced them to join the fight to take advantage of their fine horses.'

Another senior councillor added, 'The Kamboj stallions are known to be the finest in Jambu-dweep. Their men are consummate horsemen and will be a valuable asset to the Pahlav king. It is more than likely that they are also behind the small incidents along the borders of Kashyap-mir, perhaps in collusion with the Shakas.'

The king's head was swimming with all the information, but he was also excited about the opportunity the warnings offered. Since the day he had visited the final ceremony of the Ashwamedh Yagnya performed by Parshu-Raam, the desire for similar glory had filled his thoughts. It had tugged at his consciousness for weeks, waiting for him to release its spirit through his actions. Finally, he seemed to be getting the chance to act on it, and he said to the senapati, 'Prepare the troops for battle. Send the fastest bird couriers to the border posts urging them to be ready for any eventuality and tell them that help is on the way.'

'Yes, my lord.' The senapati quickly sent his second in command to do the needful.

The king further said, 'We have the strength of almost one whole Akshauhini Army, boasting skilled chariot-fighters, elephants, cavalry and infantry. Since the cavalry and infantry are quite well-prepared, they should form the vanguard. I doubt the terrain we are headed for will be conducive for elephants and chariots, so perhaps these should be stationed at strategic locations. If needed, they can supplement the efforts of the other divisions.'

He looked at his kulguru who had been an accomplished warrior once. Brahmarishi Vishwamitra nodded in approval of his strategy.

Looking at his grandson, he said, 'I agree, the latter two divisions can be positioned on the way to Gandhar and Kashyap-mir, ready for immediate deployment if necessary. I hope the cannibalistic Pishach tribes of Vahlik and the northern Hara-Huns stay out of this unholy alliance for now. The rains are still receding from the mountains and it is unlikely that we will see new troops joining them till it is completely over.' His face bore such a serious expression that Bharat was hard-pressed to remember when, if ever, he had seen him so grim.

He understood the apprehensions in his grandfather's mind and said, 'Do not worry, Gurudev, I shall leave no stone unturned in ensuring that no one can breach the sacred borders of our motherland!'

Adhyaye 30

While war clouds were looming on the horizon, Bharat's personal life was also in conflict. His mind was torn between his duty to his kingdom that demanded an heir, and the desire of his own heart.

When he thought about it, he didn't really love Jahnavi in the traditional way. Passionate, head over heels in love wasn't what characterized his relationship with Jahnavi. His understanding of love was two people who were so compatible with each other that they could look beyond their differences and help each other have a good life together.

Before circumstances forced him to go away from Hastinapur, he decided to act on his heart's desire. Who knew whether he would even return to his kingdom from the battlefield! It was better to live in the moment rather than worry about his future generations. For all he knew Jahnavi might not even agree to his proposal now.

'I spoke to my parents about us,' Bharat told her when they met again on the banks of the Ganga.

'What?' Jahnavi exclaimed in surprise, 'I didn't realize you had planned to talk about us! How did you even broach the subject?'

Bharat smiled. 'Actually it was they who brought it up, or I should say ambushed me with the topic of my marriage and very cleverly pried the information out of me.'

Jahnavi laughed merrily. 'I can almost imagine you sitting there, staring at your parents dumbfounded while they chuckled looking at each other,' she said.

'Well, it wasn't very different from how you described it,' Bharat admitted embarrassedly and waited for her to say something. When she didn't respond he decided to change the topic. 'There's trouble brewing along our northwestern border. Nobody knows if it will turn into a full-scale war yet, but the possibility cannot be denied.'

Jahnavi's heart skipped a beat when she heard about the impending war. Violence was not a way of life for the inhabitants of the underwater realms who co-existed with many other species peacefully. She knew of the wars that humans fought for land and dominance, but she could never understand why they did it. Her happy expression turned into a worried frown as she asked, 'Is it necessary to have a full-scale war that could take many innocent lives? Even if the answer to that is yes, is it necessary for you to be there? Doesn't Hastinapur have generals who could take care of such troubles?'

Bharat was touched by her concern for his safety. He looked at her with a sombre expression and said, 'It is a Kshatriya's duty to face the challenges that threaten his nation. We didn't take the war to anyone. It is the outsider, the barbarian, who has come knocking at our doors. When faced with such a situation a good king always leads from the front instead of hiding behind his generals.'

She nodded in understanding. Daman had to fulfil his Dharma, the debt he owed to society. After all, Kshatriyas were the protectors of human societies just as Brahmins were the intellectuals who gave it direction; Vaishyas tilled the lands and traded to bring in economic prosperity and Shudras formed the very foundation that enabled other three Varnas to function.

'My father is waiting for our final decision,' Bharat said coming back to the original question. 'If you say yes he shall send a missive to your father with the proposal. I hope Maharaj Sarvasen will not object to it.'

Jahnavi replied in a measured tone. 'You know, Daman, that I don't think of you as a paramour. But I will never say no to a chance of being with my best friend for the rest of my life! This is not some teenage infatuation that we have . . . it's a deeper, more stable feeling of being right for each other even though we belong to two completely different backgrounds.'

Bharat visibly relaxed. She had put into words the very thoughts that had been bubbling in his mind. He embraced her awkwardly, feeling her warmth for the very first time. They had never gone beyond holding hands before this, but she responded affectionately.

'Then it is done,' he said grinning. 'Let me return to my father and get the proceedings to begin immediately!'

'Yes, it is done,' Jahnavi said joyfully, 'though I hope you realize that I can't stay away from my natural element for too long. I shall have to return to the river every now and then.'

'Don't worry, my dear,' Bharat said. 'If need be, I'll tell the royal engineers to construct a canal connecting the palace to the river!'

Jahnavi laughed at that. Bidding him farewell she dived into the river with an excitement she had never felt before. The thought of losing him to a battle had erased any doubts she had about being with him for the rest of their lives. She had to talk to her father before Hastinapur's emissaries arrived. If nothing else worked, she would have to convince him that this was the best way to ensure the continued survival of their species!

Bharat rode back to the palace with a lighter heart and directly headed towards his grandfather's quarters. The Brahmarishi was preparing to light the evening sandhya fire and he welcomed the king with open arms.

'Congratulations, my boy,' he said, 'I am glad you came to the right decision after all.'

Bharat marvelled at his grandfather's omniscience and bent to touch his feet. 'Pitamah, your support means a lot to me! Now that I have your blessings I am not afraid of the future any more.'

Vishwamitra saw the look of relief on his grandson's face and said, 'Yes, I am with you, but I cannot promise you a future free of trouble. The problems anticipated by your parents may well turn out to be real.'

The king asked anxiously, 'Do you foresee something bad, Pitamah? I know you can see the past, present and future.'

The Brahmarishi shook his head and said, 'My boy, the day I performed your naamkaran ceremony, I promised myself that I would not divine your future. I shall help you prepare for whatever comes your way, but the outcomes of those actions remain completely your own. The Chandravansh has always remained a sanctuary for different genetic pools and your mother is a living proof of that.'

The shadow on Bharat's face lightened somewhat, but he wanted to eliminate all doubt so he asked, 'Does that mean there is a possibility that Jahnavi and I shall have a child?'

'Yes,' the Brahmarishi replied, 'there is always a chance, however remote. But if the fate gods rule against that eventuality, you know what you will have to do.'

Bharat nodded solemnly. He was the ruler of the Puru kingdom, and it was his duty to sire a strong and sturdy heir for the sake of the kingdom. If the worst came true, he would have to marry again regardless of how he or Jahnavi felt about it. As he left, the Brahmarishi gave a deep sigh of contentment. The young and impetuous Sarvadaman from the forests of Naimish-Aranya was quickly transforming into the firm and sagacious Raja Bharat of Hastinapur.

Bharat

Adhyaye 31

The marriage was fixed for the day of Ganesh Chaturthi, during an auspicious muhurat.

Bharat had wanted an understated ceremony but his mother would have none of it—she had only one child and she wanted to see him get married in a manner befitting the king of Hastinapur. Brahmarishi Vishwamitra also agreed. A grand wedding would serve two purposes: one, it would make the enemy think the Purus didn't have any inkling of their manoeuvres; and second, it would announce to the world of a powerful new alliance forged between the dwellers of land and water.

The vivah mandap, where the ceremonies would take place, was decorated with strings of auspicious marigold flowers and mango leaves. Festoons made of innumerable tiny mirrors reflected the light of the hundreds of lamps, bathing everything in a warm golden glow. The royal family began the morning by taking a dip in the holy Ganga and then participating in an elaborate Ganpati Pujan.

Brahmarishi Vishwamitra had suggested that the ceremony be officiated by Maharishi Kanav, the foster grandfather of the groom, and everyone had agreed to the suggestion. The venerable rishi was more than happy to be a part of one of the most important ceremonies of his grandson's life. These sanskars were like milestones in a person's life, beginning with their birth till the last rites on one's death, aptly called Antim Sanskar. Dressed in his usual flawless white, his long hair tied in a bun on top of his head, Maharishi Kanav took the central position in the mandap now. He invited Bharat to take a seat on the low cushioned stool placed opposite him. Between them was the Yagnya vedi, in which the Maharishi would invoke Agni, the witness of the gods, to bless the ceremony. Surrounding the two was the entire extended family of the Purus along with representatives of the underwater kingdom. Other friends of the two families had also travelled from far and wide to witness the coming together of two different dynasties in such a spectacular fashion.

Bharat looked resplendent in a purple dhoti embellished with gold thread and a mauve silk angavastra on which was embroidered the royal insignia of the Chandravanshis. The royal Puruvanshi crown had been replaced by an elaborately wound turban of the same colour as his dhoti. A glittering diamond, the size of a small ball, sat proudly on the front of the turban with a peacock feather. He wore two pearl necklaces with matching wristbands which only seemed to enhance his masculinity. His face glowed with happiness and excitement. He looked every bit the eligible bachelor that he was and many visiting princesses had envy and longing clearly reflected on their faces.

Once he had taken his designated seat, Maharishi Kanav gave him some water for Aachman. This was the first ritual in any Vedic ceremony; it involved sipping a small amount of water followed by touching all the limbs sequentially with two fingers that had been dipped in the same water. The Maharishi explained the procedure for the benefit of those guests who were not familiar with Vedic rituals especially the guests from the underwater regions.

'Aachman and anga-sparsh are symbolic processes of purification when a person embarks on a new ceremony. While touching the limbs with the holy water, we pray to the gods for physical strength and alertness and we purify ourselves to receive their blessings.'

He then invited Maharaj Sarvasen, the father of the bride, to come forward and give the groom the Madhuparka—a mixture of milk, ghee, yoghurt, honey and sugar. The king of the underwater realms had the same pale complexion as his daughter but his body was athletic and streamlined like that of a seasoned swimmer. He sported a thin moustache that curved imperiously at the ends and was dressed in regal finery and pearls. He graciously accepted the gold vessel and spoon as the Maharishi explained, 'This is not just a welcome drink as many people mistakenly believe. Since the groom is fasting before this ceremony, the mixture of these specific nutrients helps provide the energy for the elaborate rituals that are to follow.'

Bharat smiled at the words and said, 'I am more than ready for any ceremony, Pitamah. Please allow me to take this opportunity to thank Maharaj Sarvasen for this kind gesture as well as state officially how fortunate I am to have you officiate these rituals!'

The two elders smiled at the young man who was bringing the two families together. His humility and affable charm had made it difficult for Sarvasen to say no to the proposal and he had given in to the demands of his only daughter with surprising ease. The Maharishi continued explaining the procedure, 'Of the eight different ways of getting married mentioned in the Dharma Shastras, the Brahma Vivah is declared to be the best. This is where the bride and groom join in matrimony with the full consent and active participation of all family members and friends.'

He then invited the bride to the mandap. When Jahnavi arrived, led by her father, the entire venue was filled with the fragrance of wild lotuses. No one had to turn their head to know she was there, yet everyone did so to admire her ethereal beauty. Her delicate form was draped in a deep pink that matched well with Bharat's garments. The twinkle in her dark eyes was reflected in the emeralds she wore. Her hair had been tied in an elaborate plait and adorned with flowers and seashells. She had done solah shringar, the sixteen adornments a woman uses to enhance her beauty.

The Maharishi invited her to sit on the right side of the groom and handed them garlands made of roses and water lilies. She took her place gracefully and looked at her soon-to-be husband with a smile that mirrored his. They exchanged the garlands amidst tremendous applause from the guests. 'The exchange of garlands signifies mutual approval of the bride and the groom. Since they are both ready to go ahead with the ceremony, I invite Maharaj Sarvasen once again to give the hand of his daughter to Maharaj Bharat in the ritual of Pani-grahan.'

Sarvasen took Jahnavi's right hand and placed it in Bharat's. Although traditionally some of the ceremonies were meant to be performed by the bride's mother, he did them all in order to not let Jahnavi feel the absence of her mother who had died giving birth to her. The Maharishi asked him to pour the holy water kept in a vessel on Bharat's palm such that it flowed into his daughter's hand.

When this was done to his satisfaction, the Maharishi explained, 'This flow of water from the father to the daughter symbolizes the continuity of life and the passing of family heritage to the next generation. The Pani-grahan signifies the bride and groom's acceptance of their mutual relationship that allows them to pursue the three goals of a householder's life. The bride's father shall now take a promise from his son-in-law to pursue a life full of dharma, artha and kama—right conduct, pursuit of wealth, and conjugal bliss—and the groom shall repeat the promise three times.'

The two men followed the directions of the learned rishi who then asked the young king to recite a Vedic mantra,

'gribhanami te suprajastvaya hastam
maya patya jaradisthyarthasah
bhago aryama savita purandhir
mahyamtvaduh garhapatyay devah'

'I take thy hand in mine, yearning for happiness,
I ask thee, to live with me as thy husband,
Till both of us, with age, grow old.
Know this, as I declare to the gods Bhaag, Aryaman,
Savitra and Purandar,
Who have bestowed thy person upon me,
that I may fulfil my Dharmas of the householder with thee.'

Bharat delivered the prayer holding Jahnavi's hand, feeling her pulse resonate with his own heartbeat. The Maharishi asked Shakuntala to wrap a betel nut, a copper coin and some grains of rice in the corner of Bharat's angavastra and tie it to the loose end of Jahnavi's sari.

'These objects symbolize unity, prosperity, and abundance and they bind the bride to the groom. The next step is to light the sacrificial fire and invite Agni to be the divine witness of the bride and groom's transition into married life.'

The Maharishi asked Jahnavi to move to Bharat's left, indicating her transition into his family. When they had exchanged their positions, he asked Bharat to fill the parting in his wife's hair with red kumkum powder and tie the sacred necklace of black beads around her neck as a part of Mangalya Dharanam or acceptance of auspiciousness.

Shakuntala watched the ceremony with mixed emotions. She was happy for her son but she couldn't help regretting the manner in which Dushyant and she had married. 'This is how a wedding should be, with promises and vows sanctified by tradition and blessed by family,' she thought to herself. She knew the rituals were meaningless without the right intent, but they helped the bride and groom understand the significance of the social contract they were entering.

The next and final step in the ceremony was the Saptapadi in which the couple took seven steps around the holy fire and made seven vows that laid the foundation of their life together. Maharishi Kanav asked Bharat to take Jahnavi's right hand in his own and begin the circumambulation while he dictated the vows that the couple would repeat.

'O lady of my house,' Bharat requested Jahnavi in a voice full of conviction, 'the provider of life-sustaining food, please nourish my visitors, friends, parents and offspring. O beautiful lady, I take this first step with you for nourishment.'

Jahnavi responded with age-old words from the time women had taken the responsibility of managing their homes. 'Whatever food you earn with hard work, I promise to safeguard, and use it to nourish us, our friends and family.'

'O, thoughtful and beautiful lady, with a well-managed home, enable us to be strong, energetic and happy. I take this second step with you for the strength of body, character and being.'

'I will manage our home according to the best of my ability and reason. Together we shall keep a home that is healthy and energy giving.'

It was the king's turn to give an assurance. 'I promise to devote myself to earning a livelihood by fair means, to discuss, and let you manage and preserve our wealth. O dear lady, I, as Vishnu, take this third step with you for our prosperity.'

'I promise to join you in managing our wealth with mutual consideration so that it grows and sustains our family; I shall be the Lakshmi to your Vishnu,' Jahnavi replied.

'I promise to trust your decisions about the household and your choices; I vow to dedicate myself to help our community prosper. O my lady, I take this fourth step with you to participate in the affairs of our world.'

Jahnavi pledged her support in return and Bharat's face glowed with the realization that with every vow they were coming closer to becoming man and wife. He said the next words, written in the time when all men were Vaishyas and practiced agriculture to produce their own food, 'O lady of skill and pure thoughts, I promise to consult you and engage you in the keep of all our resources, cows and agriculture.

I take this fifth step with you to grow our farms and cattle together.'

'I promise to participate in protecting the cattle, our agriculture and business, all useful for our family and necessary for our happiness,' Jahnavi replied.

In the penultimate vow Bharat said with utmost sincerity, 'O lovely lady, I seek you and only you, to love, to have children and to raise a family with. I take this sixth step with you to experience every season of life together.'

The eyes of most women—and a few men—in the gathering were misty by now. In a voice choked with emotion, Jahnavi said, 'Feeling one with you, I will be the means of your fulfilment. Through life's seasons, I will cherish you and complete you.'

With a smile that extended to his ears Bharat said the final words, 'My cherished friend, allow us to cover the seventh step together, this promise of our Saptapad friendship. Will you be my constant companion?'

Jahnavi nodded as tears sprang from her eyes and she said, 'Yes, I will! Today, I have secured the most valuable friendship with you. I will remember the vows we take today and adore you with all my heart . . . forever.'

As they completed their vows, the Maharishi asked Bharat to recite another verse that described the complimentary nature of the relationship he was about to share with his better half. The king of Hastinapur dutifully repeated the words that came from his heart.

'I am the sky, you are the earth.
I am the thought, you are the speech,
I am the fire, you are the fuel.

I am the song, you are the verse,
I am the ocean, you are the shore,
I am the strength, you are the beauty,
I am the Purush, and you are my Prakriti,
Let us live together lovingly and raise our progeny,
Let us lead a joyful life of a hundred years.'

There were sounds of 'Swasti' from the gathering and the attendees showered handfuls of marigolds on the bride and the groom. They bent down to touch the feet of Maharishi Kanav who blessed them saying, 'The basis of a fulfilling married life is the physical, mental and spiritual unity between husband and wife. A man's wife is his Ardha-angani, half of his body. Marriage is not a mere state of self-indulgence; it is an opportunity for two people to grow together.'

Bharat was glad he had found the kind of caring life partner that others only dreamed of. Jahnavi too was delighted to be married to a man who loved her and respected her independence. The royal musicians began playing an uplifting tune as the guests from both above and below the land greeted the newlyweds with gifts. Shakuntala and Dushyant were happy for their son and prayed that the fear they had about his progeny would remain unfounded. Vishwamitra hoped the news of this alliance between the forces of Bharat and Sarvasen would be enough to discourage a serious attack on the kingdom. Bharat's married life had begun with a lot of expectations.

Adhyaye 32

The day went by in the various fun games and activities planned for the bride and the groom. The purpose of these was to make the newlyweds more comfortable with each other and give the bride an opportunity to interact with the family she had married into in an informal setting. By the time Bharat and Jahnavi were done with the socializing, the first prehar of the night had arrived.

It was their first night together as man and wife and they were playfully pushed into their chamber and the doors shut amidst a lot of giggling and sniggering. Finding respite after the hectic activities of the day, the two flopped down on the bed with matching sighs of exhaustion.

As they gradually relaxed, Bharat said softly, 'So how does it feel, Jahn?'

Jahnavi opened one of her eyes and replied with another question, 'How does what feel?'

'Well, you know, becoming the better half of the spoilt and pampered king of Hastinapur?'

A smile escaped Jahnavi's lips as she propped herself up on an elbow and answered merrily, 'Well, to be honest, the feeling *has* been slowly sinking in all day and I think I will probably savour being the voice of reason to my impetuous and bratty husband!'

The newly married groom sat upright and flashed his perfect teeth. Their friendship had matured on the basis of their mutual regard and affection for each other. But today, while they had been saying their vows to each other in the presence of their families and Agni, the representative of the gods, he had sensed a subtle transformation in their feelings for each other.

Jahnavi looked at his pleased expression and sat up. Taking his hands in her own, she said, 'When you proposed to me for the very first time, I hadn't been sure about turning our friendship into something different, but today, seeing the love and good wishes everyone showered on us, it feels as if we did make the right decision after all.'

'So it is just because of others' happiness that you are feeling happy?' Bharat asked.

'Well, mostly yes,' his wife replied with a serious face and added, 'but I can't deny that there is another reason for my joy. Perhaps it's the thought that I shall have you, my best friend, with me through all the ups and downs of our future.'

Bharat's face lit up at her words and he said, 'I will be with you for always and forever. I too feel blessed to envision a future in which you are right next to me, not just as a friend but also a confidante and lover.'

Jahnavi's face turned crimson with the last word and she lowered her gaze bashfully. Bharat gathered courage and raised her chin to look into her beautiful dark eyes. He cupped her face in his hands and brought her closer to him, kissing her on the forehead. Jahnavi's heart began beating faster as she leaned on his chest and he caressed her head lovingly. One by one he removed the adornments from her hair, placing them on the table beside their bed carefully. He patiently untied the flowers that had been woven into her long hair and the intoxicating fragrance of the night-blooming rajanigandha filled the room.

Bharat's breathing was becoming more laboured; he didn't trust himself to speak. He held her shoulders and made her sit straight. Jahnavi looked into his eyes without a word, then ran her hand through her long hair that was free now. A frisson of desire ran through Bharat. By the Holy Trinity, she was beautiful!

He hesitantly removed the glittering jewels that adorned her shapely neck. He took off her earrings and nose ring, unhooking them slowly and deliberately, enjoying the effect his actions were having on her. Jahnavi's chest heaved with barely suppressed desire. She realized that his touch felt different from what she had experienced before as friends. She decided to stop being a mere spectator and surprised Bharat by leaning forward and removing the gold around his neck. He in turn clasped her wrist and pulled off her bangles, taking care not to hurt her hands. As he moved to her feet, removing the toe rings and the anklets, she ran her fingers through his thick hair, savouring the moment and their building desire.

Night had set in by now and the wavering flames of the bronze lamps filled the room with a golden glow. Bharat straightened up and moved to her midriff, wrapping his hands around her waist, untying the girdle that sat above her belly button. Putting that on top of the pile of glittering jewels beside them, he ran his fingers on her soft skin, making her tremble.

Jahnavi held his shoulders and drew him near, bringing her face so close to his that they could feel each other's breath on their skin. Bharat untied her bodice and wrapped his arms around her, pulling her to him. Their heaving chests finally made contact. He kissed her mouth tentatively and as he felt her respond, went deeper hungrily and passionately. Though they were new to this physical intimacy it did not feel awkward. It was almost as if they were made for each other, two halves of one whole.

They spent the night in each other's arms, leisurely exploring each other's bodies with their eyes, fingers and tongues, fulfilling a desire neither had felt so strongly before. He was hers and she was his in every way that a man and a woman could belong to each other. They were no longer friends or partners in childhood crimes. They were man and wife now, partners in a blissful union for an entire lifetime.

Adhyaye 33

Perhaps the message that Hastinapur wished to send with Bharat's marriage failed to reach the enemy in time. By nightfall, even as Bharat and Jahnavi consummated their relationship, reports of massive raids by armed horsemen along the Gandhar border had begun pouring in.

Vishwamitra filled the king in when the council gathered once again for an emergency meeting. 'The attacking front of the marauding forces is formed primarily by the Kambojs. They have established themselves as a regional power on the southern slopes of the Sindhukush but originally belong to the region around the Vakshu river. Before they became mercenaries, they were known for the Kapishayani grapes and their delicious wine.'

Senapati Vikramjeet added, 'My king, the Kamboj tribes, after leaving the Vaishya profession, have been singularly successful in taming the wild stallions of the highlands, widely recognized as the finest horses in this part of Jambu-dweep. Because of their equestrian skills, they are now being hailed as Ashvakayans or masters of horse riding. They do not have an established monarchy and follow a loose republican confederation led by an elected

194

leader who offers their services to other tribes in exchange for gold and food.'

Bharat interrupted him. 'Senapati ji, if they are so bloody brilliant, why haven't *we* ever hired them for their services?'

Vishwamitra smiled at the way his protégé's mind worked.

The senapati replied, 'That is because we never had any expansionist plans, Maharaj. But yes, that is a thought worth considering and perhaps we can look into it once the current conflicts are resolved.'

'Coming back to the discussion, Pushkalwati, the capital city of Gandhar, is about four days' journey from Hastinapur on horseback. I believe we should head there first. Our northwestern borders are amply protected by the mountains, but there are two regions that provide a breach for invaders.'

He took a stylus and moved to the map that had been discussed earlier and now hung on one of the walls of the king's discussion chamber. 'One is the Karakoram Pass high up in the northern mountains about here,' he said, pointing to the specific locations, 'and second is the Kapish Pass that cuts through the western Shwet-Giri range of Sindhukush. Since the Karakoram is snowbound for most of the year, the Kambojs have no option but to enter through the Kapish Pass from where Pushkalwati is but a short ride away.'

Bharat studied the geography of the region and realized that the best way to stop an influx of the enemy was to station troops at a point where the invading marauders could be intercepted. When he mentioned the same to Vishwamitra and the senapati, they nodded in agreement and suggested that the outskirts of Pushkalwati would be ideal.

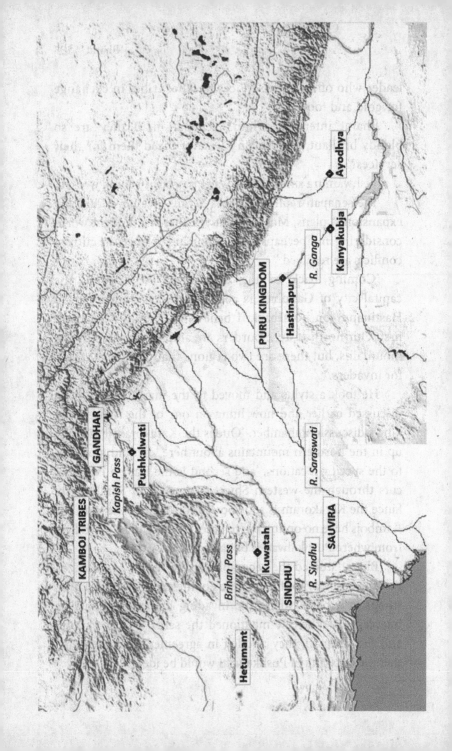

The Brahmarishi said, 'Kapish Pass is named thus because it is better travelled by monkeys than men. Rather than expose our soldiers to its terrain unnecessarily, let's wait for the Kambojs to suffer through it before facing our onslaught. The Pahlavs, on the other hand, have very wisely avoided the limitations offered by the terrain. My spies inform me that they have decided to go around the Sindhukush, bypassing the mountains altogether, and are on their way to Hariva and Shakasthan with the Parada troops.'

While the entire council reflected on this new information, Bharat's uncle Vasu said, 'They will have to fight their way through the confederacies of Hetumant to reach the Sindhu region. Our chances of catching them off guard are better than intercepting the Kambojs. The obvious choice according to me would be the Brihan Pass that cuts through the Karka mountains. It is a narrow stretch of land running through tall, rocky mountains and will severely limit the inflow of troops unless they go all the way down to the sea and come at us along the coast.'

Bharat said, 'The troops that we had sent earlier are already stationed at the city of Kuwatah. Senapati ji, please send bird couriers immediately asking them to take positions around the Brihan Pass. I would advise you to head there as well while I move to Pushkalwati. The danger is more imminent there and once I have controlled that, I shall join you in Kuwatah.'

Vikramjeet bowed his head in acknowledgment of the order and said, 'I shall be honoured to serve the Puru kingdom at the western border, Maharaj. Not that you shall need their help, but please take my excellent seconds-in-command with you for the siege in the north. A quarter of our cavalry and infantry are already stationed there. I shall send my fastest riders ahead of you to give them their orders.'

Bharat agreed to the suggestion gratefully. For all his bravado he was yet to experience a real battle and it made sense to have two experienced generals with him. 'We also have the support and blessings of Maharaj Rohitashwa. The Suryavanshi troops have been placed on maximum alert and will help us guard our eastern borders while we focus on the west.'

Vishwamitra was glad that he had taken Bharat to Ayodhya while he was a child; the friendships forged then were coming in handy now. They set about discussing the division of the troops that would allow them to send sufficient soldiers to the borders as well as leave enough to guard the rest of the kingdom.

After the discussions were over he went to meet Jahnavi. Memories of their first night together were still fresh in his mind and he longed to return to her arms. This would be their second night together, and their last before he left for the battle. The new queen of Hastinapur greeted him with a warm embrace. She was both shy and eager as he tilted her chin to kiss her on the lips. Her response made him bolder and he lifted her into his arms and carried her to the large mahogany bed. She clung tightly to him as he kissed her all over her face and neck. Their desire consuming them completely, they removed each other's clothes in earnest. They knew they wouldn't see each other for weeks, possibly months, and their frantic love-making reflected the loneliness that had already begun engulfing their hearts. It turned into a fiery passion that burnt their minds and joined their bodies as one until a final moment of ecstasy left them gasping with its intensity.

Spent, they lay wrapped in each other's arms, discussing the impending future.

'We knew what we were getting into, isn't it?' Jahnavi said, 'The very reason for our hastily organized wedding was that the enemy was knocking at our door.'

Bharat nodded slowly, playing with her hands decorated with intricate patterns of mehndi. Jahnavi spoke in a voice brimming with confidence, 'Go perform your duty as a Kshatriya and the upholder of Dharma. I wish I could accompany you but given my utter lack of military knowledge I will only be a hindrance. I shall pray to the Mother Goddess and await your victorious return just as Shachi waited for Indra's return to Swarg after defeating the dragon Vritra.'

Bharat embraced her tightly and confessed, 'Before I met you I had never felt this kind of trepidation, but ever since you've become a part of my life, the thought of not being near you makes me anxious. I shall punish the barbarians for taking me away from you and serve them a defeat they will not forget in a hurry!'

Jahnavi smiled at his declaration. Ruffling his hair, she said, 'There's the Daman I married! It is time to fulfil the name you were born with: Sarvadaman, conqueror of all. I am confident you will secure the borders of Nabhi-varsh and teach the invaders such a lesson that they will think twice before challenging our nation again.'

Even though she had said the words in full confidence, her heart worried about his welfare and she silently prayed to the gods to keep her husband safe, vowing to do so every single day till he returned safe and sound into her arms.

Adhyaye 34

By the time Bharat arrived in Pushkalwati with reinforcements, the battle had already begun.

He stood on a hillock, watching his men and the Kamboj hordes clash, getting a feel of his first battle. He wasn't a part of it yet but he wanted to observe the enemy to get a sense of their strategy before jumping into the fray. The Kamboj warriors were dressed in garments made of animal hide and fur that not only protected them from the cold winds but also provided padding against the Puru weapons.

From what he could see, the better build of their stallions was an additional advantage. The horse and the rider worked as one and he could understand why the people of the plains referred to these mountain tribes as 'horse humans'. Their banners boasted the symbol of Kinnars or Centaurs, beings with the body of a horse and the torso of a human. Vishwamitra had told him that their patron deities were the Ashwini Kumars, the twin sons of the sun god and he decided to make use of the information once he had subdued their assault.

While the Kambojs were predictable in their fierceness, the surprise element was the presence of Shak tribes amongst their forces. They wore pointed, conical headgear that gleamed in the sun and their clothes were bright red and golden.

Standing at the promontory of a small hillock with the two generals who had accompanied him, Bharat quickly began formulating a plan. From his vantage point, he could see a part of the pass that wound its way through the mountains and he realized it wouldn't be possible to hold the incoming troops at any single point. Addressing the generals, he said, 'I do not want to disengage the troops that are already in the battlefield but I can see that they are not faring too well against the Kambojs and Shaks.'

The two senior soldiers nodded grimly and Bharat said to the one standing on his left, 'General Lakshabedh, you shall reinforce them with the troops we have brought with us. I want the cavalry to surround the enemy from all sides so that the foot soldiers can fall back and tend to their wounds. Let the fight be between warriors of equal stature.'

The general nodded and quickly climbed down to relay the order. The Puru generals used a six-tone bugle signal to communicate with their troops, one specific tone for each wing of the army—the elephant masters, charioteers, cavalry and infantry—while the fifth and sixth were for the entire army to advance or retreat respectively. Within moments the command to the foot soldiers to retreat was sounded and the cavalry besieged enemy forces with fresh vigour.

The king's next command was to the other general. 'Of the two tribes the Kambojs seem to be more dangerous so let us focus on neutralizing them first. They may be excellent swordsmen, but it is also a disadvantage as they rely completely on one weapon. Our archers are the best in Nabhi-varsh and it is time to put them to good use.'

Bharat pointed to the four cardinal directions and asked for archers to be positioned there immediately. 'While our forces surround them and corral them inwards, the archers can target them easily. I want them to shoot at will. It should be easy to identify the foreigners from their distinctive clothing. Also, instruct them to avoid causing any harm to the Kamboj stallions; we'll be able to use them later.'

The general left with a nod and soon enough the unsuspecting marauders were pelted with arrows. Bharat stood still, observing the archers' accuracy and was satisfied that they were causing minimal damage to their own side. He appreciated their efforts to protect the horses as much as they could; a few stray arrows did hit the unintended but that couldn't be helped.

The sudden assault from the skies had taken the Kamboj riders by surprise but they rallied against their invisible enemies by pushing harder against the ones they could see. Bharat realized that the two armies were almost evenly matched at the moment and marvelled at the strength that the Kambojs had managed to gather without attracting any notice from the Arya kingdoms. The archers were doing their job well and had managed to stem the flow of the barbarians from the mountains but there were too many of them to be controlled for more than a muhurat. He had to end this now and the easiest way was to kill the leader of the Kambojs. He rushed down the hill and leapt on to his steed. Speaking loudly in an effort to be heard over the din of the battle, he issued orders to the commander of the foot soldiers, 'Tell your men to form a second circle outside our cavalry to take care of the enemy that has lost his mount. This shall give support to our riders and provide them some much needed relief.'

As the order was relayed he looked at the troops rushing into the melee without a care for their lives. Behind him was a force of five hundred horse riders that formed the personal bodyguard of the king; they were the finest soldiers in the Puru kingdom and it was time for them to enter the battle. He raised his voice and bellowed, 'For the moment the enemy has been trapped by our archers but there are many more behind the mountains, waiting to join their brothers. Our troops are doing a great job of neutralizing the invaders and I have no intention of letting them set foot on our holy land.'

The soldiers listened in stoic attention as he continued, 'The Kamboj chief Nasatya is being protected by a troop of giant men mounted on the tallest steeds I have seen in my life. If we can capture him, this battle will be over. We shall execute their leader and chase these barbarians back into the mountain holes that they emerged from. Are you with me?'

There was a loud roar of agreement from the troops.

Bharat asked once again, 'Are you ready to save the honour of your motherland?'

Again he got a resounding reply.

'Then ride with me today to rout the enemy that tears at our mother's breast! Death to Kamboj-adhipati!' Bharat shouted and rushed towards the battlefield. This was his first battle and he was going to crush the enemy in a way that they would never think of attacking his kingdom again.

'Death to Kamboj-adhipati!' his men echoed, riding after him.

Instead of going through the warring soldiers of both sides, he took a sharp right with half of the platoon, signalling to the rest to arrive at the same point from the other side. To the Kamboj leader it appeared that the Purus were following the same strategy as before of encircling them but that was just a ruse. The new forces were rapidly converging on his location and by the time he realized their plan it was too late to take evasive action.

The troops fell down on the leader's protectors but to their credit, the hundred odd guards were an even match for the five hundred who had followed Bharat. The Kamboj soldiers had been doing this for a living. Bharat saw each of them engage two or three of his own soldiers at once. His respect for the men grew instantly but he had to find a way past them by any means possible.

He had in his possession a wide scimitar, his favourite bow and arrow, three spears and six knives and the time had come for him to show his skills. As his forces grappled with the enemy, he manoeuvred his horse to find the gaps in their defences and shot a volley of arrows at the soldiers in the innermost circle. Some of them hit their mark and he got a glimpse of the Kamboj leader. He quickly threw two knives before the guards closed ranks; he saw them hitting flesh though his adversary didn't even wince.

Positioning his bow at an angle he shot more than a dozen arrows into the sky and as they descended in the midst of the fighting troops, multiple soldiers as well as their mounts buckled in pain. Bharat saw the Kamboj chief fall as well. This distracted the enemy soldiers for a moment and that was enough for Bharat. He leapt from his horse and sneaked into the enemy ranks. Throwing his bow down, he grasped the scimitar and ran forward. A few strides and he was face-to-face with his target but was trapped from all sides by Kamboj soldiers.

The Kamboj-adhipati was an exceedingly handsome man with a physique of a wrestler and stood one full head taller than him. He gave a loud war cry and rushed at the Puru king with a mace. Bharat parried the blow with his sword but the impact hit him hard. Nasatya was heavy and was using his body weight against Bharat but the latter had agility on his side. As the Kamboj chief rushed at him again he decided to use his enemy's own weight against him.

He turned to the side at the last moment, and the blow landed on the horse ahead of him. The poor animal neighed in agony and buckled, throwing off its rider who fell between the two fighting leaders. Instinct took over, and before he knew it, Bharat had severed the soldier's head in one stroke. This was the first time he had killed anyone and he felt numb for a moment. But he was a Kshatriya, and couldn't let his emotions overpower him.

The Kamboj chief charged at him again. This time he stood his ground, blocking the blow with his own sword. Killing the soldier had sent the adrenaline surging through his body and he pushed the Kamboj king with all the strength he could muster. Sparks came out of the weapons, and in spite of his smaller size, he managed to topple his adversary and strike him with the pommel of his sword.

Nasatya fell and his grip on the mace loosened but he kicked Bharat in the shin and made him tumble. The Puru king steadied himself, taking the support of his sword and lashed at the Kamboj with his feet. By this time, all the Kamboj guards had either been overpowered or struck down; the earlier circle around the fighting leaders was now entirely composed of Puru soldiers. The Kamboj chief flung his mace and grabbed the sword of one of the fallen soldiers to cut

Bharat deep on his arm. The sharp pain jolted Bharat and filled him with anger. He had never felt this kind of hatred for any man before and he channelled all his rage into destroying the man who had dared to attack the sovereignty of his nation.

With a loud cry, he launched himself at his opponent. They came at each other with swords and then with bare hands but none could better the other. Finally, tired of the tussle, Bharat hit Nasatya's face with his elbow, breaking his nose. The Kamboj chief's vision blurred and blood gushed from his nostrils as he crumpled to the ground in agony. Taking advantage of his position, the Puru sovereign hit his face with his knee, further smashing the delicate bones of the nose. The Kamboj was now struggling to draw air through all the blood that was filling his airways and Bharat stopped, moved by his plight. He was a king, not a murderer and would not kill an enemy who was already gasping for his life.

This was a fight between the civilized and the barbarian and he would set an example for his soldiers in upholding the Arya code of conduct even while battling the enemy. He stepped away from the leader, and ordered his guard to take him captive.

Adhyaye 35

The battle on the outskirts of Pushkalwati sealed the victory for the Purus at the northern border and the victors had marched to the capital city of Gandhar with the prisoners in chains.

After the defeat of their leader, the Kamboj troops surrendered unconditionally. They were mercenaries after all and their own lives were more valuable to them than someone's imagined cause. Bharat had counted on this when he targeted Chief Nasatya and his gamble had paid off. He had ordered that the prisoners be held at the fort in the Gandhar capital for the time being and left half of his cavalry there while the rest of the Puru army marched to intercept the second assault of the enemy.

According to latest reports brought by the kulguru's spies, the Pahlavs and the Paradas had managed to subdue the principalities of Hetumant and were rapidly advancing towards the Brihan Pass.

Senapati Vikramjeet, who had come to Kuwatah directly from Hastinapur, was apprising him of the details, 'The Pahlav army is almost completely composed of horse riders who wear distinctive bronze and iron chainmail. Their peculiar armour covers both the horse as well as the rider and even though it offers them immense protection, it also makes it easy to identify them. They are so confident in their defence that they don't even carry shields. The Paradas bear the sigil of the Swastika on their shields and their stallions are not protected.'

While Bharat absorbed this information, the senapati continued, 'As anticipated in our earlier discussion, the Brihan Pass seems to be the perfect place to trap the enemy.'

The king's thoughts went to the discussion that was held in the royal sabha just a few days ago. Standing in the barren landscape of the northwest, covered in dust and sweat, it seemed to him as if it had taken place a lifetime ago on a different planet. He forced his mind to come back to the present and heard the senapati say, 'The road through this pass is best suited for camels. Our enemy is riding on horses so they will find the terrain difficult to negotiate, especially after the recent bout of rain that has come without warning for us as well as them.'

'Excellent!' Bharat said. 'Now I understand why we have hardly faced any troubles on these borders before. Nature has been kind to the Arya nations and has helped preserve us from the barbarian hordes for a long time. But now that these Mlecchas are here, let us exploit the topography to our advantage.'

Vikramjeet nodded and the king explained the strategy that he was formulating after seeing the terrain. 'The mountainsides seem to be close to a hundred feet tall. That is a boon for us. Equip our foot soldiers with rocks and station them all along the pass and as far into the mountains as possible. Each infantry man should be accompanied by an archer in an alternating chain that should come unbroken right up to the opening here. We had allowed the enemy safe passage at Kapish Pass but not even a single barbarian should be able to step on our soil this time.'

The senapati acknowledged his command with a nod. 'We shall bury the invaders in such a rain of stone and metal that they will long for a glimpse of their own cities after that. They have unleashed a trail of destruction right from their homeland to Hetumant, destroying, pillaging, raping and murdering innocents and it is time someone put the fear of Yama in their hearts!'

The stratagem was executed without a moment's delay and horses were used to carry men, food and water as well as arms to the mountains surrounding the pass. There was enough steel in the hills that day to perhaps cause a change in the earth's gravitational field and Bharat was pleased with the progress they had made. According to the spies, the invaders were still half a day away by the time the Puru troops had taken up positions all along the outcrops till about half the length of the pass.

Bharat had ordered them not to go all the way to the other end since that would discourage the enemy from entering the pass in the first place. His plan was to let the entire unsuspecting force of the barbarians enter the narrow pathway and then trap them in the tunnel of rock. It was almost evening by the time the first Pahlav soldier was seen riding into the tunnel.

When it seemed like more than half the troops had entered the pass an owl hoot echoed through the mountains—it was a signal amongst the Puru soldiers indicating that their prey had arrived. The Arya code of conduct forbade any warfare after sunset but the invaders were not bound by it. Their plan had been to storm into Puru territory and wreak havoc on the towns and cities even as their occupants slept peacefully.

Unfortunately for them, Bharat believed in paying the enemy back in his own currency. He had ordered the soldiers to thwart the attack no matter the time. He himself stood at the mouth of the pass, leading the cavalry in case any of the barbarians managed to get through. As the owl-hoot reached him he gave the signal to the generals to begin the onslaught. Immediately the hills erupted in loud cries of 'Jai Bhavani' as the Puru soldiers began their assault.

Within moments rocks began raining on the Pahlavs and Paradas, followed by sharp arrows that found their mark even in the rapidly declining sunlight. An avalanche of metal and rock had descended on them and their horses, confused by the sudden onslaught, buckled down, throwing their riders. The Pahlav king who was leading the charge realized their dilemma and ordered a retreat. But it was too late; too many of them had entered the rocky tunnels and there was not enough room for them to turn around.

Bharat knew that the looming darkness would make it difficult for his marksmen to find their targets so he had asked for the arrows to be dipped in oil and lit before firing. As nightfall descended on the confused barbarian hordes, it seemed as if the entire sky was punctured by tiny meteors that were headed their way. The Paradas saved themselves using their shields but the Pahlavs were not so fortunate. As the small twigs and shrubs along the path caught the flames from the arrows, the terrified horses ran amok, tossing their riders to the ground. Bharat ordered his soldiers to let the animals come through the narrow passage but not a single soldier was allowed to pass. The few who tried to escape by riding through were immediately slaughtered by the Puru cavalry. In spite of their superior armour and planning, the invaders were experiencing the same dance of destruction that they had unleashed on unsuspecting populations before.

It was all over within the prehar and after the last armoured horse ran towards them, the Puru soldiers rushed in with torches to look for anyone who may have survived the assault. Bharat had ordered the capture of all injured soldiers and animals while those who had died in the onslaught were to be burnt inside the passage that had already caught fire at multiple places from the Puru arrows.

It was time for the king of Hastinapur to celebrate his first victory. Bharat stood on a rock and congratulated his troops. 'It hasn't even been a fortnight since we left Hastinapur, yet we have managed to crush the barbarians' attack. I salute the valiant soldiers of the Puru army who have defended their motherland so bravely from the Mlecchas of the west.'

There were lusty cries of jubilation and he let his men savour the moment. When the intensity of their shouts abated, he raised a hand to quieten them and said, 'Sadly, we also lost many of our brothers, especially in the battle outside Pushkalwati. To honour their memory, I hereby announce the construction of victory pillars at Kuwatah and Pushkalwati with the names of the martyrs engraved on them. These will not only remind us of their great sacrifice but also deter the enemy from ever returning through these routes!'

There was loud applause at this. The senapati was impressed by his king's perspicacity. For a soldier, dying for his motherland was the only reward he sought, but it did gladden his heart to see that the citizens he was protecting were grateful to him for endangering his own life to save theirs.

Bharat looked at the captive leaders of the forces that he had defeated and further declared, 'The Pahlavs, Paradas and their supporting Yavans are denied entry into Nabhi-varsh for all time to come. They have shamed their patron deity Mitra, the god of friendship, by their actions and there is no room for such barbarians amidst the genteel populations of our great nation. The Shaks of the north are also denied any trade exchanges or personal visits to Nabhi-varsh. The borders of Puru shall be closed to them for all eternity.

'As for the Kambojs, they have showed exceptional valour in the battlefield, and I applaud the strength of their chief, Nasatya. I have decided to offer them clemency and induct them into our army. They shall be stationed at the southern border of Puru where a new settlement shall be constructed for them. I respect their beliefs and intend to build the largest temple dedicated to the Ashwini Kumars in this part of the world.'

The applause from the soldiers was considerably lacking in enthusiasm this time but the senapati and the generals welcomed Bharat's decision heartily. The induction of such skilled soldiers into the Puru cavalry would not only boost the forces for the kingdom but also promote healthy competition between the soldiers. Besides, their allegiance to the Puru kingdom would ensure a steady supply of the prized Kamboj stallions. The king had also cleverly stationed them away from their homeland so that they would not be able to plot against him ever again. They would be in an alien land, spending most of their time adjusting to the different food, language and climatic conditions. Raja Bharat was fast turning into a force to be reckoned with.

Adhyaye 36

After his consecutive victories, Bharat decided to take a long tour to secure the entire border from the west to the north. Giving the orders for the construction of the Vijay Stambhs, he asked the Kamboj chief Nasatya to accompany him to the northern reaches of the Himalayas. The grateful leader of the horse warriors had sworn undying loyalty to his new master and took him to places that Bharat could have never accessed by himself.

Together, they subdued the Daradas, the wild tribes living north and northwest of Kashyap-mir and their king, Achalamangala, accepted Puru suzerainty, offering vast quantities of rare precious stones that were sent back to Hastinapur on the backs of two-humped camels. Bharat spent a few days in the beautiful valley named after Rishi Kashyap whom he had met years before at the Ashwamedh Yagnya organized to mark the end of Parshu-Raam's campaign. The scenic valley surrounded by the mighty Himalayas made him miss Jahnavi and he sent courier birds to her, saying he would join her soon.

Riding down with the combined forces, he conquered the territories of Kaikeya, Madra and Trigarta watered by the tributaries of the Indus. Thereafter, they crossed the Saraswati, moving towards the Matsya kingdom that was their immediate neighbour to the west. Easily subduing the half-hearted efforts of King Virat, he appointed a Puru representative there and gave orders to start the construction of a highway connecting Kuwatah to Viratnagar, the largest city of the region.

He visited the kingdoms of Sindhu and Sauvira whose kings, aware of his recent victories over the barbarians, readily accepted his overlordship, extending the Puru command to beyond the banks of the Indus. Vikramjeet wanted him to remove the kings and place his own men in their stead but Bharat refused and explained, 'Senapati ji, politics turns into just a diversion for the trivial mind if not played with skill and finesse. If we don't take calculated risks from time to time we are no more than boys with false bravado trying to become men.'

From Sauvira, he sent a major section of the army back to Hastinapur while he himself rode on with his generals and his personal guard to Kanyakubja where his young cousin Yaudheya, Vishwamitra's grandson, now ruled, and negotiated formal terms of peace with him. It was almost five months by the time Bharat returned to Hastinapur and was warmly welcomed by his family.

Dushyant and Shakuntala beamed with pride and kissed his forehead as the erstwhile king said, 'I had expanded the boundaries of my father's kingdom from Ganga to the Saraswati and now you have taken it further to beyond the banks of the Sindhu river! Truly this is the best gift a Kshatriya son can give his father.'

Bharat touched their feet and took their blessings before retiring to his chamber to meet his beloved wife. Jahnavi embraced him tightly, the desperate longing in her heart finally appeased. As her eyes roved over him, hungrily taking in every detail, she noticed the changes that had occurred in his body. His skin had tanned and his muscles had become heavier, testament to months of hard labour. He sported long hair and a beard. The man who stood in front of her looked very different from the boy who had left her days after their wedding, but when he kissed her, it was with the same warmth and concern for her as before. Bharat also noticed the change in his wife's body and she confirmed his suspicion—she was expecting his baby! The news brought tears of joy to his eyes and he held her close and they fell asleep in each other's arms.

Jahnavi let him sleep for the rest of the day as well as night. When Bharat finally opened his eyes it was already next afternoon. He was supposed to address the royal assembly that day. As he watched his wife give orders to the attendants to bathe the king and dress him in the regal robes he had not worn in months, he became acutely aware of the difference between his life as a king and that as a soldier. It felt strange wearing the finery. There was once a time when he had enjoyed the touch of the soft fabrics and the glitter of the diamonds that came with his position as a prince but now, after living in the harshest terrains of his kingdom, he realized how superfluous all these adornments were.

The royal court was bursting with citizens who wanted to offer their good wishes to the king. When he entered the hall, Bharat was greeted with an unprecedented display of affection. He took his place on the moon throne and sat down with folded hands to acknowledge their wishes. The kulguru, who stood to the right of the throne, brought order to the crowd and said, 'On behalf of the citizens of Puru, I extend a warm welcome to our liege and protector and congratulate him on a successful campaign against the barbarians of the northwest. I also thank each and every soldier who has sacrificed his family and his life to safeguard our nation.'

Vishwamitra looked at his grandson with undisguised appreciation and pride. 'Since your arrival, the Tushars of Tarim and the Rishikas of Asii have sent you offers of peace. After hearing of Maharaj's victories, our southern neighbour Avanti, has also expressed its willingness to cede to the power of the Purus. They have already volunteered to hand us the town of Ashmak on their southern border for settling the Kambojs.'

Turning to the citizens thronging the hall he said, 'Due to our king's efforts, the Puru Empire today extends from the Sindhukush mountains in the west to Mother Ganga in the east. Our southern boundaries are marked by Godavari while only the Himalayas keep us from conquering the Mlecchas of the cold deserts.'

Bharat's heart filled with love for his people as the chants of 'Long Live Raja Bharat' echoed in the hall. Amidst the encouragement the Brahmarishi said, 'Only five rulers in the present Manvantar have managed to expand their kingdoms to a considerable extent: Maharaj Prithu, who gave his name to the planet; the Suryavanshi emperor Mandhata; our very own Chandravanshi ruler Maharaj Yayati; I, as the king of Kanyakubja, and the unfortunate Kartavirya Arjun. None of us however belong to Puruvansh. Let us all hail the first ruler of Puruvansh to hold sway over such a large tract of the nation!'

As the court erupted in cries of joy once again, Bharat smiled at the words of his grandfather. Even though he did not belong to the Puru linage, Vishwamitra's loyalty to the house was beyond question. He thanked him as well as the crowd that had gone berserk and declared a week of celebration for the entire kingdom.

Later, when he met the Brahmarishi separately, Vishwamitra told the king about his parent's plans to take Vanprasth. Bharat was sad at the news but he knew they had to follow their own path in life. The Brahmarishi also told him that his adopted son Devrat, who had been married a few months before Bharat, had sired a baby boy who had been named Yajnavalkya.

Bharat was pleasantly surprised with the information. Since he had taken over the reins of the kingdom he had hardly been able to spend time with his adoptive uncle who had busied himself with the pursuit of Brahma-vidya. He made a mental note to visit and congratulate him and his wife after meeting his parents. The news of Devrat's baby also brought to the fore fears about any children he and Jahnavi may have. He shrugged the thoughts away and embraced his Pitamah happily; he would take life one step at a time.

Coming back to the affairs of kingship, the kulguru said, 'Now that our western and northern boundaries have been secured, we have also received support from the central kingdoms. But trouble is brewing on the eastern borders. I have with me a request from Rohitashwa asking for your help.'

Bharat was worried for his friend. 'When did this arrive, Pitamah? Why didn't you send me a courier?'

Vishwamitra replied gravely, 'I didn't want to disturb your consolidation of the northwestern territories. I have however taken the liberty of turning back the troops Ayodhya had sent for our protection. That should have boosted their defences for the time being. Now that you are here, you can decide if you want to go to your friend's aid yourself.'

The king nodded in understanding. As kulguru, his grandfather's primary responsibility was towards the Puru kingdom and he wouldn't compromise on that. But Rohitashwa was a dear friend and he had to help him in his time of need.

He quickly made up his mind and told the Brahmarishi, 'Please ask the senapati to prepare the troops that we had stationed in and around Hastinapur. It is time these men got a chance to earn some glory while the other battle-weary soldiers rest and recuperate. We leave for Ayodhya in three days.'

Vishwamitra immediately called an attendant to send the message to Senapati Vikramjeet. 'But are you sure you don't want to spend some time here before you leave?' he asked, concerned. 'It has been a long time since you were in the capital, and it will do you good to get some much-needed rest.'

Bharat shook his head and said, 'My rest is not as significant as the need my friend has, Gurudev. Please tell me what you know about the enemies he is facing right now.'

The Brahmarishi answered the question bubbling in Bharat's mind and said, 'Do you remember our discussion regarding the kingdoms of the east? Beyond Kamarupa, Sonit and Lauhitya, are the lands of Kiraats. They live in the forests as hunters and are known for the elaborate traps they lay to capture big prey. At present they pose no threat to us but they have forged an alliance with the Chins and the Hara-Huns against the kings of Anga and Vanga. Rohitashwa, being the latter's ally, has gone to help them but finds his armies spread out too thin.'

The king understood the quandary that his friend was in. 'I am glad you sent their forces back, Pitamah, they needed them more than us. Bhrata Rohit stood by us when we needed assistance and as Ayodhya's allies, it is our duty to help them now. Please tell me more about these barbarians of the east.'

'The Kiraats are degraded Kshatriyas like our cousins in the west. Although they worship Lord Shiva, their beliefs lie more towards Animism and Shamanism. Animism is the idea that each living or non-living entity contains a powerful spirit that can help or hurt us, and Shamanism involves gaining control over these spirits to perform superhuman or supernatural acts. The Kiraats are being instigated by the Chins and Hara-Huns, tiny little devils who live further to their north. They fight with short daggers, blunt stones and bamboo canes, and pack a mean punch.'

Bharat stopped walking and asked his grandfather, 'Why are all these tribes focusing their attention on Nabhi-varsh right now? At the same time as the barbarians in the west?'

Vishwamitra sighed and replied, 'Your cousin Raam had effectively subdued the barbarians for a long time. Before him, they were under the rule of Kartavirya Arjun. As Menaka pointed out on her last visit, both these men belonged to Nabhi-varsh, so it is natural for the people of these kingdoms to have some resentment against our nation.'

'But these people are barbarians, aren't they? Isn't it the duty of all Kshatriyas to spread the beacon of civilization to the world?' the Puru king asked, perplexed.

The kulguru smiled and said, 'I myself have believed that all my life but with age I am coming to realize that war is not the only way to do that. We can use other means to change the hearts of the tribes who live a more primitive form of life. Education is one option. In the current scenario, however, exerting force to defend our borders is completely justified. Both these clans, even though Manavs, are no better than the Rakshas tribes living in Lanka. They eat anything that crawls, walks or swims, and are even known to consume human foetuses!'

He shook his head in disgust and said, 'The Chin king Dhautamulaka is hungry for power and he looks towards our fertile lands to extend his dominion. The Huns are no more than nomads who wear crowns of animal skulls and kill other tribes for fun. They have to be driven back for the sake of preserving Manav Dharma.'

That night, and for the next three days, Bharat spent as much time as he could with his parents and Jahnavi. She wasn't prepared to let him go so quickly again but she also knew that there was little she could do to stop him from helping his friend. The responsibility of the realm now lay heavily on his shoulders . . .

Adhyaye 37

When Bharat arrived on the scene he realized that the very thing that had worked for him in the west was now favouring the intruders from the east. With the help of the northern barbarians, the Kiraats had conquered Kamarupa, Sonit and Lauhitya and were now breaching the borders of Anga and Vanga in a multipronged attack.

Bharat met the kings who had sought his help to decide the strategy for the battle. Rohitashwa, the king of Ayodhya, was leading the discussion. 'The first step is to secure the borders,' he said, 'You have managed to do that for the time being but your soldiers can't be stationed at the border for all eternity. What happens if the kings on your western borders decide to take advantage of the situation?'

Prasenjeet, the middle-aged king of Vanga, protested, 'Magadh and Videha will never do that to us!'

Rohitashwa countered with a question, 'I hope they don't, but the question is *what if*? The Kiraats, Chins and Hara-Huns will keep your men tied up for the better part of a year and that is long enough for someone to figure out the opportunity it provides. We can't leave your citizens at the mercy of their goodwill now, can we?'

The thought of being attacked from *two* sides put Prasenjeet and Gaurang, the teenage king of Anga, in a worried state so Bharat sought to break the tension. 'Well, now that we know the problem, let us focus on the solution. We have to take the kings of Magadh and Videha into confidence right now and ask them for help in the name of patriotism for Nabhi-varsh.'

'What if patriotism isn't enough?' asked the young Gaurang.

Bharat responded with a grim smile, 'It better be; they are sandwiched between Bhrata Rohit's Kosal on their west and your kingdom in the east.'

'Kamarupa, Sonit and Lauhitya have already been ravaged and their forces commandeered by the Kiraats,' he continued. 'The only thing keeping the invaders from the rich Gangetic plains is the defence offered by the two of you. We have to make Magadh and Videha realize that and convince them to add their forces to yours for the sake of keeping the barbarians out of our hallowed land.'

Rohitashwa marvelled at the deep understanding of statecraft Bharat had developed in such a short time. He smiled and patted Bharat's back. 'I am so proud today to see my young friend give such sage advice to his seniors! No wonder you managed to convince the kings of Sindhu, Sauvira and Matsya to follow your leadership.'

Gaurang nodded and said, 'If our combined forces win the day, I pledge my undying loyalty to the houses of Ayodhya and Hastinapur. Anga will be honoured to accept your suzerainty and become a protectorate.'

Rohitashwa said, 'Ayodhya does not differentiate between its own house and that of the Purus. Whether Suryavanshi or

Chandravanshi, we all belong to the same motherland. We are happy to back Hastinapur to take the lead in this matter.'

Bharat was overwhelmed with the offer. Not even in his wildest dreams could he have imagined that the prince whom he had looked up to as a kind of mentor and elder brother would one day be willing to choose him as his emperor. But he replied to both with folded hands, 'My friends, I do not require any inducement to help you! We fight together as protectors of Nabhi-varsh and to free our brothers and sisters in Kamarupa, Sonit and Lauhitya from the clutches of these eastern barbarians.'

King Prasenjeet folded his hands in respect and said, 'This is not a bribe. You have shown us the vision of a strong nation ruled by one ruler once again. I witnessed the reign of Kartavirya Arjun that spread from Avanti to the whole globe. I also saw its downfall due to the emperor's attachment to power. You have the opportunity to change the fate of Aryavarta with the voluntary acceptance of those you are leading.'

Bharat was honoured by their belief in him but he knew it put a huge responsibility on his shoulders. He bowed to all three in gratitude and said, 'We can discuss this *after* we have defeated the invaders. For now, let us try to persuade Videha and Magadh to help their brothers in need. My own forces are already spreading in between yours to strengthen the defences.'

As he slept that night, exhausted by the negotiations, Bharat's mind plunged into a deep abyss. He tossed and turned in his bed, in the forlorn hours of the night, his subconscious mind trying to find its way through a quagmire of self-doubt. He had put on a brave face for his peers but he was still just a young man who was taking each day as it came. True, he had tasted success in the very first campaigns he had undertaken, but what if it was just beginner's luck?

He slipped into the state between deep sleep and consciousness, and saw himself floundering in the wilderness. He was alone, with neither soldiers to protect him nor family to comfort him. A dense fog began rolling down the hillside, engulfing him in its wispy arms and a hungry wind began rummaging through the landscape, rustling up dry leaves and lashing out at creaky doors.

Fear clutched at his heart. Stumbling over rocks and brambles, he spotted a flickering source of light. It was a torch, mounted on a pedestal, braving the winds to shed its meagre light upon the surroundings. As he lifted it cautiously, his gaze fell on a heap of decaying human bodies, hugging each other in a macabre display of intimacy. He gasped and hastily stepped back, shutting his eyes against the sight.

After a moment, he opened his eyes and turned his attention to the twisted corpses again. The light from the torch pierced the darkness like a warm blade through butter and he breathed in relief as he realized that the bodies were actually gnarled roots of dead trees. Suddenly he saw something move within the twisted mass of dead wood; he wasn't sure whether it was a trick of his mind or a play of light and shadow. He was in the middle of a vast wasteland and the tangle of ancient growth looked like a primeval octopus waiting to pounce on him. A sudden neighing sound shattered the silence and out of the darkness emerged a snow-white steed, galloping towards him. As Bharat stood stock-still, wondering what to do, the animal slowed down as it approached him and came and stood right in front of him. Dropping the torch on the ground, the Puru king swiftly mounted the horse. He was just thanking the gods for their timely assistance when a creeper from the overhanging canopy twisted around his neck and lifted him off the horse, leaving him dangling in the air as the animal bolted out of sight.

He was swaying to and fro in the air, struggling to keep the vine from suffocating him, when an arrow sliced through the creeper, releasing him from its vicious grip. He fell down with a thud, coughing and panting for breath. Looking around, he saw a dark girl dressed in rough clothes, wielding a bow, an amused expression on her face. Her dreadlocks were spread around her head like a halo and a garland of skulls dangled from her hip. Even before he had processed the image of this huntress, she pointed an arrow right at his heart. Smiling seductively, she beckoned to him to get up and run for his life. He did not know what other option he had and began to sprint away from her while she chased him as if he were a hunted animal. Ducking below branches and jumping over the dense bramble he finally heard the sound of an arrow being released from a bow and turned around in surprise.

The next instant the arrow had pierced his heart.

Bharat woke up with a start, clutching his chest in agony. He was actually experiencing the pain and it seemed as if his entire left arm was throbbing with it. There was a squeezing sensation in his chest and jaw and he couldn't breathe. He tried to shout for help but no sound came out of his mouth. His body broke out in a cold sweat and he struggled to get on his feet. His dream had been so real that his brain was finding it difficult to separate illusion from reality. It was a big day for them and he could not let anything distract him. Yet his body felt leaden, sluggish, following his commands after a delay of a few moments. He knew something was terribly wrong and remembered his grandfather. The Brahmarishi possessed many Siddhis and could travel with the speed of thought and sure enough he saw Vishwamitra standing in front of him within a heartbeat.

The Brahmarishi helped him sit up in bed. 'I know the confusion in your mind, my son,' he said, pre-empting Bharat's questions. 'It was witchcraft.'

'What!'

'Yes, my child. The eastern barbarians are known for their practice of the forbidden arts. Their use of dark magic is another reason I had compared them to the Asurs earlier. It is the same darkness that destroyed the lives of my nephew Yamdagni and his wife Renuka but I will not let it affect you in any way.'

Seeing Bharat's turmoil, the guru explained, 'Your presence in the region must have upset the barbarians and they tried to get into your head. The natural trepidation in your mind was multiplied manifold by their sorcerers to make you believe in the false reality they created. So much so, that when the personification of Kali, the goddess of destruction, shot you in the heart, your mind registered the pain as real and put you in a limbo.'

Bharat was fascinated by his grandfather's words and realized that there were many more things in the world for him to discover. To clear his confusion he asked, 'Does that mean my mind and body shall take time to recover normal function?'

'They would have,' the Brahmarishi said, 'but now that I am here I'll help you get rid of the numbness.'

He asked his grandson to close his eyes as he kept a hand on his head and whispered a mantra. A few moments later, when Bharat opened his eyes the sluggishness was gone and he felt absolutely fine. He began to thank the Brahmarishi, but was forestalled.

'Don't thank me yet. There's a lot more that can happen during the course of tomorrow. I shall stay here for some time and provide you the protection of pure Brahman magic so that you can focus on the task at hand.'

Adhyaye 38

The next morning, Vishwamitra asked Bharat to get ready and go out to meet his allies.

The couriers that had been sent to Magadh and Videha the previous day had returned with good news and the combined forces of the six kingdoms would be led by the Puru king. They were able to control the foray of easterners into new territory but the defences that the Kiraats had put were proving difficult to breach. The barbarians had dug up trenches and laid elaborate traps in them, lining them with wooden logs that ended in sharp points. Many soldiers of the allied forces lost their lives to these treacherous traps. There were three layers of such extensive digs and beyond them were waves upon waves of bloodthirsty soldiers ready to ravage the bountiful kingdoms of Nabhi-varsh.

Bharat knew he had to quickly find a way to break the impasse before the morale of the citizens of the three kingdoms trapped on the other side gave way. Since the forces on land were not proving sufficient he decided to use the underwater platoon of soldiers he had put together with the help of Maharaj Sarvasen. Calling an emergency meeting, he informed the other kings of his decision, 'The combat-ready divers thrive in amphibious conditions, and can fight on land as well as under water, having been trained by the best soldiers from my wife's city.'

There were murmurs of approval as he continued, 'Please order all your archers to keep the enemy engaged with an incessant rain of arrows so that my elite force can dive into the Brahmaputra undetected and swim through the enemy's defences. Once they have crossed into enemy territory they will spread out all along the length of the river and launch an attack on the enemy from behind.'

The orders were carried out immediately and the archers of the three kingdoms, supplemented by a few troops that had begun arriving from the western neighbours, blotted out the eastern sky with a shower of arrows that forced the enemy to retreat. The well-trained commandos of the amphibious force took refuge in the deep waters of the river and Bharat dived along with them to give them direction. He was as comfortable under the raging river as the soldiers and there was no way he would let them enter the fray without leading the way himself. Each of the fifty soldiers carried a small, light shield and two sharp daggers that could not only injure the enemy but also cut through the thick hide of the crocodiles or alligators who populated the river, if required. They swam together silently, barely causing a ripple on the surface and, taking one last deep breath, dived under the wooden barricades erected by the enemy. Once they were through to the other side, they could see the arrows shot by their own soldiers tearing through the water all around them.

The archers of the allied forces were inflicting immense destruction on the enemy and he could hear the muffled sounds of hurt men and animals through the water. They had to get past the range of the deadly missiles so Bharat signalled them to quietly continue their progress till they had gone a fair distance. Once he was sure they were clear, he signalled the men to start fanning out to both sides of the river.

The men spread out along the bank and broke the surface gently to replenish their parched lungs. When he was sure that all of them had taken their fill of the life-giving oxygen, Bharat gave the order for the attack. The mixed Kiraat, Chin and Hara-Hun troops were taken by surprise and within moments the commandos had annihilated all those who dared to cross their path. Their own archers had been given the orders to stop firing after a muhurat and Bharat started pushing the enemy towards the barricade they themselves had created, sandwiching them between the allied forces on the other side and his own men behind him.

Emboldened by the external support they were getting, the captive soldiers of the three subjugated kingdoms also rebelled and for the first time in the history of Nabhi-varsh, the forces of the eastern kingdoms fought as one. The strategy proved to be a success, and after a day of intense fighting, the allied troops were able to shatter the enemy defences and mete out a humiliating defeat.

But it appeared that the enemy wasn't going to give up so easily. A dark cloud was forming on the horizon and Bharat could see a full orange moon rising behind it. Suddenly a mournful voice rent the air; it was as if someone was dying. Tired and exhausted though he was, Bharat was perplexed by the sudden change and his suspicions were roused immediately. This was no natural phenomenon, he could feel it in his bones. The hairs on his arms prickled and a sense of foreboding engulfed him. He saw the same reaction on the others' faces and quickly remembered his grandfather.

The ground beneath their feet began to tremble as if during an earthquake. The horses and elephants scattered in panic and so did the men, abandoning whatever they were doing. Bharat, who was leading his men on foot, saw a decomposing corpse float towards him. It was followed by another and another till he was surrounded by the stench of putrefying death.

Within a fraction of a second he felt the reassuring hand of Vishwamitra on his shoulder and he breathed a sigh of relief. Addressing all of them, the Brahmarishi said, 'This is the dark magic of the barbarians. Your unexpected victory has rattled them so badly that they have stooped to this level. Their Shamans practice necromancy to predict the future but turning the dead into slaves is going too far.'

He spat in disgust at this repugnant use of the forces of nature. Closing his eyes, he raised his arms to the heavens and summoned the power of the Gayatri Mantra. There was an answering flash of lightening followed by a loud thunderclap. Bharat looked at his grandfather and guru who was lost in a deep trance and was glad they had him on their side. A protective cover of pure Brahman energy, crackling with blue electricity, was forming around the army and Vishwamitra cautioned everyone to stay within it. 'These barbarians are abusing the powers of nature to serve their twisted agenda. But do not worry, I am with you and I won't let any harm come to anyone.'

'Gurudev,' Rohitashwa came forward and bowed to the Brahmarishi. 'How can we sit back and let you do all the work? Undoubtedly, you are more than capable of handling any dark power, but please tell us how we can aid you!'

Vishwamitra smiled at his eagerness and replied, 'As you wish, Rohit! I am turning your weapons into celestial arms that can cut through any kind of dark magic. Make good use of them. May the gods be kind to these unfortunate souls!'

'That's more like it,' said Bharat.

The soldiers' spirits lifted immediately. They could fight any enemy as long as it belonged to the realm of the known. They had been momentarily stumped by the appearance of the floating corpses. But now, with the blessings of Brahmarishi Vishwamitra, they wouldn't hesitate to destroy these phantasms. A sudden bright light blinded them momentarily, but when they opened their eyes, they saw that their weapons were glowing with the same blue power that surrounded them.

Within a few moments the air was rife with the acrid smell of burning flesh. Every time a weapon sliced through a corpse it caught fire and turned into ash. Vishwamitra looked around and saw that the army of zombies was being neutralized effectively. Heartened by their success, the kings mounted their steeds and, together, the forces of Anga, Vanga, Videha, Magadh and Ayodhya, led by the Puru, chased the invaders across the Arakan range that formed the natural boundary between Nabhi-varsh and the eastern regions.

Bharat was emboldened by their victory and told his grandfather that he now wished to tour the southern kingdoms before returning to Hastinapur. Vishwamitra's shrewd mind registered the fact that after this immense show of power, no one in their right mind would challenge his grandson's right to be crowned the emperor of Nabhi-varsh.

Adhyaye 39

As the sun went down the horizon on the most important day of her life, Jahnavi sat on the steps leading to the river, overwhelmed by grief.

She had sent Bharat to the battlefield the first time, nine months ago, with the hope that he would come back to her once the rebellion on the western borders had been crushed. But he had proceeded on a prolonged tour of the northern and western kingdoms before returning. Then he had followed his friend Rohitashwa into the eastern kingdoms which had taken almost a month. She had hoped he would come back for good after that victory, but instead of returning home, her husband had then led the Kamboj troops stationed in Ashmak to conquer the southern lands.

Bharat had been notching victory after victory and she was happy for him, but she hadn't seen him in months, barring the three days he had spent with her. She had spent the entire duration of her pregnancy without him by her side, and today, when they should have been celebrating the birth of their first child, she felt completely lost and alone.

After nine months of a gruelling and complicated pregnancy, she had birthed a child who had unfortunately not survived. The baby was born with fused limbs, much like the fins of a fish, and couldn't breathe for more than a few minutes. Her heart had shattered into a thousand pieces when she held the lifeless body of her newborn in her arms. Shakuntala and Menaka had been there for her but what she had needed were the comforting arms of her husband who was yojans away. Her mother-in-law, while trying to console her, had told her that this was a possibility she had communicated to their son long before the wedding, and though Jahnavi knew Shakuntala meant well, the knowledge broke her completely. Succumbing to the myriad emotions tormenting her, she had shut herself to the outside world.

As she sat on the steps now, her tears seemingly spent, the door to her chamber flew open with a loud bang. Wild-eyed, dishevelled, Bharat stood in the doorway, desperately looking for her. The moment she saw her husband, grief overwhelmed her once again and she burst into fresh tears. Bharat ran to her and took her in his arms, holding her in a tight embrace. The sobs racking her slender frame reverberated through his body as well and brought tears to his eyes.

'I am so sorry I was not here for you, my love,' he said in a choked voice. 'I should have been here for you throughout this period but . . .'

Jahnavi's grief turned into anger at his words and she asked indignantly, 'Why weren't you here, Bharat? Why *did* you leave me alone to deal with this?'

Bharat hid his face in her neck and let his emotions out for the first time. 'I couldn't bear to see my parents' prediction come true, Jahnavi!'

Jahnavi was stunned by his answer.

'I was hoping that somehow my staying away from Hastinapur, setting the wrongs in the world right, would help change my karma and give us a healthy child. The gods wanted Nabhi-varsh to become a beacon of civilization in this world and I hoped that by fulfilling their wish I would be able to change my fate!'

His words affected Jahnavi in a way she could have never imagined. She raised his face which was more weather-beaten than ever and looked into eyes that were brimming with unshed tears. She saw his honesty reflected in them and felt her anger melting away.

Bharat was still speaking. 'I wished to conquer all of Nabhi-varsh, from the Himalayas to the southern ocean, and gift a stable empire to our child but I failed. I have come back as the king of the civilized world but have lost the child for whom I did all this!'

They embraced each other in mutual misery, letting their grief flow through their eyes. After some time, when they had both gained some control over their emotions, Bharat said, 'Jahnavi, you are the only person I look forward to having in my future. My parents had told me that there is a possibility that we might not be able to have children, but when you conceived, I thought the worst was behind us. Perhaps I should have told you this right in the beginning, but I did not want our married life to be overshadowed by thoughts of an uncertain future.'

Jahnavi gave him a sad smile and asked, 'So you decided to bear the burden all by yourself? Why didn't you marry someone else, Bharat? We could have remained friends all our lives and you could have married a princess worthy of you, one who would have given your kingdom an heir.'

Fresh tears sprang from her eyes as she realized without his saying what he had done for her. Her husband was a man of principles and he would never have thrown her over because of a shortcoming. That knowledge made her love and respect him even more. They were soulmates, meant to spend their lives together and they wouldn't let the lack of children destroy their relationship.

Bharat stroked her head softly and said, 'Your love was the only thing that kept me going through the lonely nights spent in deserts and snows. Whenever a stray breeze carrying the fragrance of wild lotuses reached me, I wanted to abandon everything and run back to your arms. But I persevered to please the gods and hoped they would spare us this agony.'

'Well, you are back now,' Jahnavi said sagaciously, 'and I hope you are planning to stay. I need your presence to feel secure and wanted again; I need you to help me forget the past nine months as nothing more than a bad dream; I need your hands to hold mine whenever I start spiralling down a vortex of self-pity.'

'I am here, my love, and shall be with you the rest of my life,' Bharat promised squeezing her shoulders. 'Unless of course, I need to teach the barbarians another lesson in the future!' he teased.

'No, not even then,' Jahnavi said petulantly. 'From now on, I shall accompany you wherever you go.'

He nodded and kissed her on the lips to seal his promise. As the scarlet sky began darkening in anticipation of the moon's arrival, he let his emotions flow from his heart. He remembered his childhood that was spent in the forest, training with his pet lions as a teenager, diving into the cool waters of Ganga with Jahnavi, watching the stars glittering in the firmament on warm summer nights . . . The thoughts filled him with a deep melancholy.

They gazed at the full moon together, each absorbed in their own thoughts. Jahnavi was the love of his life, and he couldn't bear to see her hurt like this. An idea was forming in his head. 'Jahnavi, what if this is exactly the way things were meant to happen?'

Jahnavi didn't understand what he was saying so he explained, 'What if we were never meant to have a normal baby? Should we ask Pitamah for help? Perhaps he can conduct a Putra-kameshthi Yagnya for us . . .'

'What are you saying Daman I can't understand any....' Jahnavi was about to ask him again what he meant when the truth hit her. Perhaps the reason they could not have a child themselves was that the empire Bharat had built required an heir of more-than-human calibre.

She thought about it for a while and finally nodded, tentatively. She had heard of other land-dwelling kings who had performed such sacrifices and obtained illustrious heirs from the gods. Bharat relaxed at that. They had suffered a great personal loss, but perhaps this would turn out to be the happily ever after they had been waiting for.

Adhyaye 40

The Brahmarishi could not have said no to his grandson even if he had wanted to. But he did confess that given his history with Indra, the yagnya would have to be performed by someone other than him for the gods to be truly munificent to them.

He recommended they ask Maharishi Bharadwaj, the son of Devarishi Brihaspati, the chief preceptor of the gods, and the stepbrother of their erstwhile guru, Acharya Dirghatamas. The Maharishi had been raised by the storm gods, the Maruts, who were close attendants of Indra, and his officiation of the Puru ceremony could help in influencing the decision.

Bharat was extremely impressed with the pedigree of the Maharishi so Vishwamitra advised him to head to the ashram of the rishi in Prayag and invite him himself.

As the decision was conveyed to the royal family, a wave of elation filled the palace of Hastinapur once again, replacing the gloom that had enveloped them in the past few days. The entire city came together to organize the grand yagnya that their king had planned. They had never been a part of such a grand ceremony and volunteered in large numbers to help with the arrangements. Sages and magi were invited from all over the country to be a part of this monumental event. A huge tract of land was cleared to set up the massive marquee required for the ceremony and arrangements were made for rishis who would be chanting mantras to support the efforts of the chief priest. Enormous quantities of the usual sacrificial offerings were procured— camphor, fresh fruit, betel nut, saffron, kumkum, turmeric powder, sandalwood paste, marigold flowers, mango leaves, coconut fruit, plantain shoots, ghee, milk, and holy water from the Ganga.

By the time Bharat and Jahnavi returned with Maharishi Bharadwaj, all the arrangements had been finalized.

Maharishi Bharadwaj had inherited his father's molten gold complexion and fiery looks but there was a cool, composed aura about him that Bharat found comforting. He bore no resemblance to his half-brother Dirghatamas. His gold-tinged hair was piled on top of his head, and his thick beard and whiskers gave him a commanding appearance that was in contrast to the sagacious and benign expression of the erstwhile kulguru. The Maharishi sent the royal couple for a cleansing dip in the river, and then set about preparing the yagnya vedi with the help of the other rishis who had arrived and were awaiting his instructions.

Changing into fresh clothes, Bharat and Jahnavi took their positions at the yagnya vedi. In order to be considered complete and meaningful, all Vedic sacrifices for householders required the presence of the man and the woman of the house. After two prehars of continuous pouring of oblations and chanting of mantras, there finally seemed to be a change in the character of the flames leaping from the vedi. As the

Maharishi poured the last oblation for the prehar, there was a gushing sound, like that of a raging waterfall, and a small tornado began forming within the confines of the yagnya vedi.

Bharat and Jahnavi were alarmed and inched backwards but the Maharishi stayed them with a raised hand. Addressing the gathering in a booming voice, he said, 'The gods have accepted your offerings, Maharaj Bharat. I can feel the presence of my foster fathers in this vortex of energy.'

A hush fell on the gathering at the realization that none other than the storm gods, the Maruts, were arriving amidst them. Most officiating priests would have invoked Agni, the god of fire for this yagnya, but Bharadwaj, having been raised by the Maruts, had invoked his parents to fulfil the wishes of his patron.

Maharishi Bharadwaj addressed the tornado of pure energy that was rising high towards the heavens while remaining confined to the limits set for the sacrificial fire. Folding his hands in a gesture of supplication, he said, 'Beloved fathers, your adoptive child requests your presence in this sacrificial arena. Pray, show yourselves in this holy fire and fulfil the desire of this righteous king.'

The hurricane of energy began transforming into a giant face that was composed of multiple smaller faces that spoke together in a deep rumble. 'Ayushmaan bhav! Long live our child!'

Bharat remembered that the Maruts were forty-nine in number. The crackling and glowing face of fire addressed him directly this time, 'We, the Maruts, know the deepest terrors of every living being. We rage through land and water, touching the lives of many creatures, putting the fear of the lord in their hearts.'

Fascinated, Bharat watched the multiple faces talk simultaneously as though in one voice, in perfect cohesion. 'We are dreaded by everyone and never in our long lives, have we been asked to bless someone with good fortune. Aawah, Prawah, Udwah, Samwah, Viwah, Niwah and Pariwah—all the seven groups of Marutgann have come here to see the person who has organized this astonishing ceremony. Our hearts are filled with elation at this thoughtful gesture initiated by you as the patron of this yagnya. Ask, and you shall receive that which even the fate gods hadn't planned for you, O king and queen of Hastinapur.'

Bharat and Jahnavi bowed their heads, secretly delighted that their decision to approach Maharishi Bharadwaj had paid off, and folded their hands in salutation. The queen didn't trust herself to speak; her entire body was trembling with the realization that she was in the presence of some of the oldest Vedic deities. She urged her husband to convey their gratitude and voice the request on their mind appropriately.

Bharat gave her a look of assurance and replied to the Maruts in a tone that rang with sincerity, 'O exalted and ancient beings, I cannot adequately express how grateful I am to you for heeding our call and arriving in our midst. Born from the womb of Mother Diti, you are seven times seven yet one in spirit. You left the Daitya way of life to help Indra uphold the balance of good and evil. What more can I ask for save your blessings that will enable us to continue maintaining the same equilibrium here on Prithvi.'

The patchwork of faces smiled in appreciation and another rumbling voice boomed across the arena, 'Your quest is a noble one, O Puru king. We know the pain of being childless and the fulfilment one experiences with siring a child. Bharadwaj is not our biological son but he is ours in all but name. Born of Devi Mamta and Devguru Brihaspati, he carries on the good work of all his ancestors and we know you too desire an heir who can take your legacy forward.'

Both the king and the queen nodded eagerly and the voice said thoughtfully, 'The lives of all mortals are filled with irony; even those of the gods. We, the Maruts, have never created a child of our own, content as we were with the love and affection of Bharadwaj. Yet, today, we create a child with the consecrations of all forty-nine of us, but we do not keep it for ourselves.'

All of a sudden, the intensity of the energy column increased and the whirlpool of fire began rotating again. The crowd waited with bated breath for what would happen next. Jahnavi's heart was beating like a drum. After what seemed like an interminable wait a sound pierced the hush that had fallen on the gathering—a baby's first wail!

The column re-arranged itself into the forty-nine faces and the echoing voice announced to the eager king and queen, 'This child, born of our essence, we now give to you. Raise him as your own flesh and blood, for he shall be the king of all the lands that he sets foot on and shall be known as Bhu-manyu.'

Out of the raging fire emerged two hands that placed a healthy, glowing baby in the lap of the trembling queen. Jahnavi couldn't believe that the fates had finally smiled on her and presented her with a child to rear as her own. As she held the infant close to her chest, she was struck by the thought that this was no ordinary child, but the benediction of some of the most ancient gods. In one graceful stroke they had fulfilled Bharat and her deepest desire and flooded their lives with happiness.

Bharat wiped away the tears that sprang from her eyes. 'This is the time for happiness, my dear,' he said. 'We have received that exceptional grace of the gods that few even dare to dream of. Let us forget the past and start a new life for our family.'

While his misty-eyed parents smiled, the tiny miracle cried its heart out, oblivious to the happiness his existence brought to the heart of every single person in the gathering. Bharat realized that the gods had blessed him with the most suitable candidate to rule the nation that he had united. The citizens of Hastinapur showered flowers on the royal family, celebrating the advent of the heir to the moon throne.

After the ceremony was over, Bharat touched his parents' feet and took their blessings. Dushyant and Shakuntala had been waiting for the birth of their grandchild and now that they had beheld him, they would soon move to the forests for the next stage of their lives, relinquishing all their worldly possessions.

Bharat went to meet his grandfather who had deliberately stayed on the periphery of the procedure. The Puru king's heart was bursting with gratitude. Before he could say anything, however, Vishwamitra enveloped him in a tight embrace.

'You are an exceptional boy, Bharat,' he said, 'and the choices you have made in your life are all testimony to that. Congratulations on becoming a father!'

Bharat gave his grandfather a boyish grin that reminded Vishwamitra of his mischief as a child. His eyes misted with nostalgia but he shrugged the feeling away. He was a Brahmarishi, a conqueror of desires; such a show of weakness was for householders, not ascetics like him. He apprised his grandson of the far-reaching ramifications of the grand yagnya.

'All of Nabhi-varsh is buzzing with talk of the ceremony. All the rishis who had come from different corners of the country are spreading the word about the special benediction that the storm gods have bestowed on you. Your acceptance of a child who is not your own as the leader of your people has also set a new benchmark for other kingdoms—only the most deserving candidate can become the king! Did you know, in honour of the man who has united the entire country under a single banner, they are calling our great nation Bhaarat-varsh now?'

Bharat was stunned by the news and protested fiercely. 'But Pitamah, I do not deserve such an honour!'

'Who other than you deserves it more, my boy?' the Brahmarishi asked with a smile. 'Your leadership has brought together the kings from Sindhu-Sauvira to Sonit and Lauhitya. It is your name that is honoured today from Kashyap-mir in the north to Kanyakumari in the south. In the current Manvantar, there has not been any single person who can match your valour and compassion. The honour that your subjects bestow on you is well deserved!'

When the bewildered expression on his grandson's face didn't change, the Brahmarishi sat down with a sigh and said, 'Let me tell you a story.'

Bharat recognized the stubborn set of his grandfather's face and decided against arguing with him. He sat down with an expression of resignation. Vishwamitra began the narration with a question, 'Do you remember our lesson on Maharaj Nabhi, who gave his name to the nation?'

Bharat nodded solemnly and the guru said, 'Maharaj Agnidhra, the ruler of the entire planet, had apportioned Jambu-dweep amongst his nine sons and our country, located south of the Himavat mountains, was given to Nabhi. The king, who was married to Meru Devi, the daughter of Indra, sired the great renunciate, Rishabh, who is also considered an incarnation of Lord Vishnu. When it was his turn, Rishabh Dev had a hundred sons, the eldest of whom was Bharat.'

This last bit piqued Bharat's interest. 'He had the same name as me?'

The Brahmarishi nodded, and continued, 'When he renounced the world, Rishabh Dev distributed his kingdom amongst his hundred sons just like his father. Bharat received the city of Ayodhya that had been established by the first man, Manu. Being ambitious, he did not wish to settle for just a city when he could easily conquer the world. He embarked on a long journey of world domination in which he was immensely successful. The only people remaining for him to subdue were his younger brothers.'

In spite his initial scepticism, Bharat found himself engrossed in the story.

'King Bharat demanded absolute submission from his brothers. Ninety-eight of them agreed but one did not appreciate the subordination expected from him. This was Bahubali, who challenged his eldest brother to a duel. The world was witness to a fierce fight between the two brothers, a fight that set the tone for all future sibling rivalries because of its intensity and far-reaching consequences.'

'But who was the winner?' Bharat asked restlessly and Vishwamitra replied with a smile, 'Your namesake of course; that is why I am telling you this story.

246 Dr Vineet Aggarwal

'The eldest son of Maharaj Nabhi became the indisputable lord of the entire world. People began referring to the entire world as Bhaarat, or the domain of Bharat. But when his brother Bahubali knelt in front of him along with the other ninety-eight brothers, Bharat did not experience the feeling of jubilation he had been expecting. His mind was berating him for having subjugated his own siblings to fulfil his ambitions and with this epiphany, that comes from a great life-changing experience, the king of the world decided to renounce all that he had won.'

Seeing Bharat's surprise, Vishwamitra added, 'The lord of the world had come to the same realization that once helped me attain the title of Brahmarishi, and has also made your cousin Parshu-Raam famous. Conquering the physical world means nothing, if one does not have control over his desires.'

Smiling broadly, the Brahmarishi declared, 'You, my child, possess that same insight that made your namesake turn into a saint. The Vishnu Puran recorded his feats and credited him for uniting the entire world under his banner and you must strive to be remembered in the same way. If *you* do not deserve the honour of having the country named after you, no one else ever will! Our part of the world crashed into Kimpurush-varsh some sixty million years ago, giving rise to the Great White mountains that separate us from the rest of the world. This piece of land has always stood out from the others; history will forever remember it in your honour as Bhaarat-varsh.'

Epilogue

He lay on the gargantuan coiled body of Shesha, the serpent of time. A golden dhoti was draped across powerful legs while his muscular body glowed with the effulgence of Brahma-jyoti. The Kaustubh gem glittered on his neck, resting beside the garland of vaijanti flowers while the handsome head rested on one of his arms. Ringlets of dark, curly hair spilled over his broad forehead, framing high cheekbones and lotus-bud eyes. Eyes that were observing the developments on Prithvi, while the Milky Way swirled around his abode in Dhruv Loka.

Shri Hari Vishnu was happy about the way things had turned out in Nabhi-varsh. Bhaarat-varsh now, he mentally corrected himself. He loved the new name as much as he loved the boy who had given his moniker to the mortal nation. Manavs were so full of promise! Shri Hari Vishnu enjoyed following their lives, especially of those whose acts outshone those of others around them. Even though their lifespans were shorter than his single breath, yet in their own trivial ways, they made a difference to the collective destiny of mankind.

He knew that in the future Bharat would perform a thousand Ashwamedhs and a hundred other yagnyas to honour the gods using the expertise of exalted souls like Bhrigu, Kanav,

Vishwamitra and Bharadwaj. He would conduct Agnishtoma, Atiratra, Uktha, Vajpeya and Vishwajeet yagnyas—sacrifices that many kings on the mortal plane hadn't even heard of. Following the directives for just rule laid down by his cousin Parshu-Raam, he would look after his citizens like his own children and distribute so much in charity that future generations would wonder at his magnanimity. No one had performed such feats in the past, and nor would anyone do so in the future. He might even help the Devas in their eternal battle with the Asurs. Humanity would face many new challenges in the times to come. Ravan, the half Rakshas-half Brahmin great-grandson of Brahma, was on the verge of having his prayers answered. Another boon given by one of Vishnu's counterparts would necessitate his intervention once again in the affairs of the humans. This time he would have to be more actively involved. Vishwamitra had told Bharat that the story he wanted to share about Vishnu's divine bow was still in the future, and that time seemed to be arriving quickly now.

But till then, Bharat's legacy would endure and keep reminding mankind of its potential. Srishti—creation, Sthiti—equilibrium and Samhar—annihilation would continue in a never-ending cycle. The future was built on the ashes of the past, and he, Vishnu, the Preserver, would make sure that that balance never faltered till the end of time.